*What could be hotter than a cowboy in June?
How about a cowboy in July, August,
and under the mistletoe, too!*

New York Times bestselling author Vicki Lewis Thompson is back in the Harlequin Blaze lineup for 2014,

and this year she's offering her readers even more....

Sons of Chance

Chance isn't just the last name of these rugged Wyoming cowboys—*it's their motto, too!*

Saddle up with

#799 RIDING HIGH

(June)

#803 RIDING HARD

(July)

#807 RIDING HOME

(August)

And the sexy conclusion to the Sons of Chance series,

#823 A LAST CHANCE CHRISTMAS

(December)

Take a chance...on a Chance!

Blaze®

Dear Reader,

I support animal rescue organizations no matter what species they're rescuing. Although my favorite shelter these days is The Hermitage No-Kill Cat Shelter in Tucson, I've also volunteered at Best Friends Animal Sanctuary in Kanab, Utah, where they take in almost any creature, including potbellied pigs!

I had an up close and personal experience with these adorable creatures, and yes, one of them was named Harley. The real Harley is way better behaved than the fictional one I created for this story, but how else was I going to arrange that first kiss between Regan and Lily without a misbehaving pig? And you know there will be lots of kissing and...other stuff, because we're starting a whole new summer of the Sons of Chance!

I've had *such* fun with this series, and apparently, so have you, so here we go again! Take one equine veterinarian who craves order, and one genius-level woman determined to save every animal on the planet and let them do whatever they choose, and you have a beautiful mess. Throw in the Chance family, who can be helpful or meddlesome, depending on the circumstances, and you have *Riding High*. I can't wait for you to read it! You're gonna love those pigs.

Charitably yours,

Vicki

Vicki Lewis Thompson

—

Riding High

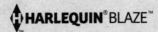

HARLEQUIN® BLAZE™

Recycling programs
for this product may
not exist in your area.

ISBN-13: 978-0-373-79803-2

RIDING HIGH

Copyright © 2014 by Vicki Lewis Thompson

Printed in U.S.A.

ABOUT THE AUTHOR

New York Times bestselling author Vicki Lewis Thompson's love affair with cowboys started with the Lone Ranger, continued through Maverick and took a turn south of the border with Zorro. She views cowboys as the Western version of knights in shining armor—rugged men who value honor, honesty and hard work. Fortunately for her, she lives in the Arizona desert, where broad-shouldered, lean-hipped cowboys abound. Blessed with such an abundance of inspiration, she only hopes that she can do them justice. Visit her website, www.vickilewisthompson.com.

Books by Vicki Lewis Thompson

HARLEQUIN BLAZE

Prologue

June 10, 1990, Last Chance Ranch, from the diary of Eleanor Chance

THANKS TO MY grandson Nicholas, we have another orphaned puppy ensconced in the boys' room upstairs. Nicky calls him Hercules, and he's supposed to stay in his box because he's not housetrained yet. The whining has stopped, so it's a safe bet the little bugger's in Nicky's bed. Mark my words, we'll be washing sheets in the morning.

I know it's foolish to imagine what profession a child will take up as an adult, but I'm convinced that Nicky is going to be a vet. Yes, I realize he's only eight and boys his age change their minds on a regular basis. One day they want to be a firefighter, and the next they'd rather drive an eighteen-wheeler, or maybe fly a jet.

Nicky's different. He brings home enough strays to start a shelter if we were so inclined. But that's not why I figure he'll end up running a veterinarian clinic when he grows up. Half the time the animals he rescues have some injury or other. This puppy has a torn ear and a limp, and instinctively, Nicky knows what to do. It's remarkable for a boy so young.

Henry Applegate, our large-animal vet from Jackson, makes regular visits to the Last Chance, and Nicky follows him around like a rock-star groupie. He watches every move that man makes and asks so many questions it's a wonder Henry doesn't complain. I guess he's flattered that Nicky idolizes him so.

Fortunately Jonathan and Sarah are encouraging this interest. Jonathan agrees that his middle son has a gift, and Jonathan's already hoping that Nicky will one day take over the medical care of the Last Chance horses. Personally, I'm glad there's at least one steady boy in the batch.

Jack, the oldest, has a wild streak and is guaranteed to turn his father's hair prematurely gray. Gabe, the youngest, is the most competitive kid I've ever known. Jonathan plans to enter him in cutting-horse competitions when he's old enough. Now that school's out for the summer, Gabe's driving us all crazy setting up contests of every kind. Yesterday it was rope climbing. Today it was an obstacle course. Thank God he doesn't expect me to participate! I could probably climb that rope and navigate the obstacle course, but I'd rather not find out I couldn't. Now that I'm almost eighty, I prefer to maintain my illusions.

Whoops, gotta go. Nicky's calling for us. He says Hercules peed in his bed. Now there's a shocker.

1

Present day. Shoshone, Wyoming

DEAR GOD IN HEAVEN. Regan O'Connelli, DVM, parked his truck outside the large double gate of Peaceful Kingdom Horse Sanctuary, nudged his Stetson back with his thumb and leaned his forearms against the steering wheel while he contemplated the sight before him. If his hippie parents ever ran an animal rescue operation, it would look like this.

Nick Chance, his brother-in-law and business partner, had mentioned that Lily King was slightly…different. Judging from the psychedelic colors she'd painted the ranch house, the barn and the outbuildings, *different* was an understatement. Even though he was wearing his Ray-Ban sunglasses, the neon green, pink, orange and turquoise hurt his eyes.

She had to be the one who'd chosen the color scheme. She'd taken over from an elderly couple two months ago, and prior to that, it had been too cold to paint. Maybe if she'd stuck with one color per building, the effect wouldn't have been so startling. But a pink barn with turquoise doors and trim was wrong on so many levels. It was a wonder the horses agreed to go inside.

Or maybe they'd refused. He counted at least twenty of them milling around the property, which was a dozen more than Nick had told him to expect. There was a corral—he could see it from here—but the gate was open—accidentally or on purpose? He had a feeling she'd meant to keep it open so the horses wouldn't feel constrained by any artificial boundaries. His parents would have done that sort of thing, too.

Regan wished Nick had given him a little more information before sending him off on this mission of mercy. All he knew was that Lily's parents were two of Nick's favorite high school teachers and their daughter had an extremely high IQ, although she'd never stuck with one major long enough to earn a degree when she attended Berkeley. She had, however, invented a video game that continued to pay royalties, and she'd wanted to do something charitable with the money.

Maybe Nick had been vague about Lily's free-spirited persona because he knew Regan's history. Regan and his seven siblings had lived a vagabond existence with their parents, traveling the country in a van painted the same colors Lily seemed to favor. Nick wouldn't want to make fun of Lily's setup and insult Regan's folks in the process.

Everybody at the Last Chance Ranch had come to love his unconventional parents, Bianca Spinelli and Seamus O'Connor. Regan loved them, too, even if they had saddled their kids with the surname of O'Connelli to avoid hyphenating O'Connor and Spinelli. They'd also given each child a gender-neutral first name to prevent stereotyping. Grade school had been hell, especially because the family had moved constantly and the name thing had to be explained every time they'd enrolled somewhere new.

Regan had forgiven his well-meaning parents long ago, but Lily's paint job brought up memories he'd rather forget. He had a job to do, though, and the color of the buildings had no bearing on that. Nick, who'd invited Regan into his vet practice six months ago, had volunteered out here for several years when the Turners had run the place. Nick had said he was grateful Lily had come along. Without her sudden decision to buy it, the sanctuary would have closed.

Regan agreed that Lily was performing a valuable service, so he was prepared to do his part. As he climbed out of his truck and closed the door, a second truck pulled up. He didn't recognize the middle-aged couple inside, but he instantly identified the crated animal in the back of the truck.

When the man left the driver's seat and started toward the tailgate, Regan walked over to find out what was going on. "Looks like you have a potbellied pig there."

"Yes, sir, I do." The man adjusted the fit of his ball cap. "If you wouldn't mind, I could use a hand carrying the crate. My wife helped me get Harley up there, but I think she did something to her back in the process. Harley's put on a lot of weight since we got him."

"They tend to do that." Regan made no move to help with the crate.

"We didn't figure on him getting this big. When he was little, we'd let him in the house, but now he's even too big for the patio. We like to barbecue outside in the summer, and with Harley's mud hole expanding by the day, it's impossible."

Regan's jaw tightened, although he knew this kind of thing happened all the time. People saw a cuddly baby animal and took it home while conveniently forgetting that baby animals grow into adults. "Where are you taking him?"

The man looked at Regan as if doubting his intelligence. "Isn't that obvious?"

"Not to me. This is a horse sanctuary, and what you have there is a pig."

"True, but I know for a fact the lady running the place accepted a pig last week from a guy I work with. So if she took one pig, I imagine she can take another. I'll make a donation to the cause. If you'd grab one end of the crate, I'd be much obliged."

"Before we do that, let's make sure she'll take him." Regan didn't know a lot about animal rescue, but asking first seemed like common courtesy.

"She'll take him. My buddy said she's a softie."

Regan held on to his temper with difficulty. "She may be, but if there's a potbellied-pig rescue organization in the area, that would be a better place for Harley."

"Look, mister." The man's eyes narrowed. "This is the day I set aside for handling this problem. My wife and I managed to get the pig into the crate and into the truck, which wasn't easy. If you're not gonna help me with the crate, step aside and I'll do it myself, although God knows what that'll do to *my* back."

"Hey, guys, what's up?" On the far side of the gate stood a young woman of medium height with the kind of bright red hair that made people take a second look. It was so kinked it fanned out like a lion's mane. Unlocking the gate, she stepped out and refastened it. She wore a tie-dyed shirt knotted at her waist, faded jeans and scuffed boots.

Regan told himself to ignore the cuteness factor as she walked toward them. Nick could have mentioned *that,* too. Or the fact that sunlight made her hair glow. Maybe happily married Nick didn't notice those things anymore. "Lily King?"

"That's me. I'll bet you're Regan, the vet who moved here from Virginia. Nick said you'd be coming today instead of him."

"Right." At her approach, his senses went on alert. She smelled great, like a fresh meadow, and as she drew nearer, he noticed the freckles scattered across her nose, as well as her intensely blue eyes fringed with pale lashes. No makeup to speak of. It should all add up to wholesome, but instead she looked sexy and approachable. Good thing he wasn't in the market right now. "Listen, this guy has a potbellied pig he wants to—"

"So I gathered." She glanced up at Regan, laughter in her gaze, as if they shared a secret.

Oh, yeah. Sexy lady. And he didn't think she was trying to be, either, which made her all the more interesting.

"And I could use a *hand* with the *crate,* people." The man had adopted a martyred tone.

"I'll help you." Lily started toward the tailgate.

"Hang on a minute." Without thinking, Regan grabbed her arm and felt her tense. He released her immediately, but not before feeling firm muscles under her sleeve. This was no delicate flower. He admired that. "Is there a potbellied-pig sanctuary where he could go, instead?"

"There is, but last I heard they're at capacity. I already have one pig, so—"

"Told you," the guy said to Regan, folding his arms and looking smug.

"So I think Wilbur would be happier if he had a friend," Lily said. "I'm willing to take this pig."

Regan accepted defeat. "In that case, I'll help carry him."

"Thanks." She gave him a brilliant smile. "I'll get the gate."

Moments later, the crate was inside the chain-link fence that surrounded the approximately five acres of her property and the couple had left without making the donation the husband had promised. Regan wasn't terribly surprised. "Where should we take him now?"

"I'll let him decide where he wants to go."

"Maybe that's not such a—" But she'd already unlatched the crate and Harley burst forth in an apparent frenzy of joy. The horses trotted out of his way, and he flushed several chickens, which rose up in a cloud of feathers and angry clucking.

Chickens?

Lily smiled as she watched the pig cavort. "See how happy he is?"

"You have chickens?"

She shrugged as she continued to follow Harley's progress with her gaze. "It's the new thing to get chickens and have fresh eggs every morning. Urban farming is very in. But when the thrill is gone, people don't want those chickens. I've had a few people ask, and I've got room, so why not? Oh, look. Here comes Wilbur to see his new friend."

Regan watched as a considerably smaller potbellied

pig came around the end of the ranch house and approached Harley. "What if they fight?"

She laughed, and the warmth of that laugh said a lot about her. She was obviously an optimistic soul who believed everything would turn out well. "Then you and I can wade in and separate them, I guess. But they're not going to fight. They like each other. See? Is that sweet or what?"

He had to admit the pigs seemed okay with each other, but it could have just as easily gone the other way. Then one of the horses, a sway-backed buckskin gelding, walked calmly past the pigs and began munching on what was left of a flower bed in front of the ranch house porch. "You let him do that?"

"If it makes him happy."

"Then I guess you don't care about having plants there."

She turned to face him. "I took over the sanctuary because I want to give these horses a home and a sense of self-worth. If they want to eat the flowers, so what? They've been arbitrarily yanked away from the life they used to know, so they deserve to be spoiled, right?"

"Philosophically, yes. Practically, no. These are two-thousand-pound animals, and they need to live by a set of rules. In fact, all domestic animals function better that way." Kids, too. He and his siblings had been given more freedom than they'd known what to do with. Somehow they'd avoided the serious consequences of that freedom, but he shuddered when he thought of how their lives might have turned out.

"I disagree." She said it cheerfully, though.

"Is that why you don't have the horses confined in the corral or the barn?" Or did the horses stage a rebellion when they caught a glimpse of that pink-and-turquoise monstrosity? The jury was still out on how well horses could see color. At the moment Regan wouldn't mind a little color blindness, himself.

"Exactly. I let them wander as they wish, and they all show up in the barn at mealtime. When it's cold, they tend to stay in there during the night, but they're welcome to go wherever they want on the property."

"Makes my work more complicated if I have to chase them down."

She nodded. "That's what Nick said. He'd rather have them all in one place when he comes out, and I meant to close them in the barn while they ate breakfast. But the sunrise was so beautiful that I got distracted. Before I realized it, they'd all eaten and headed out. Once they're loose, it's nearly impossible to get them in again until dinner. I should have arranged for you to come before mealtime, instead."

"Next time I'll do that." He sighed. "Guess I'd better get started."

"I'll help, but I wonder if…"

"If what?"

She hesitated, her expression earnest. "Would you consider, just this once, rescheduling for this evening?"

"Well, I—"

"Never mind. That's asking too much. You probably have a wife or a girlfriend who expects you for dinner."

"I don't, but that's not the issue."

"And there's the matter of making a second trip. I'll help you catch them and we'll get 'er done. I know I'm too lax with them, but I think about the fact that the poor things have never been in charge of their lives, and that's why I like to give them more control over their comings and goings. I promise next time I'll remember to keep them in the barn when you're due to arrive."

He gazed into her solemn blue eyes. Only a man of stone wouldn't warm to the compassion shining there, even when he knew she didn't have the faintest idea how to run this operation. "Have you spent much time around horses?"

"Not until I took over the sanctuary, which was a leap of faith. I wanted to come back home and do something good for the community, and this place really spoke to me. Now I'm around horses 24/7."

Déjà vu. Either of his parents could have delivered that kind of speech, except that none of their seat-of-the-pants decisions had involved horses.

"And you know what?" Her expression grew more animated. "They're such individuals! Buck, the one who likes to eat the flowers, is really stubborn, while Sally, that little bay mare over there, is shy. You have to coax her to be friends, but once she trusts you, she'll follow you around like a dog. I have to watch out she doesn't try to come in the house."

Oh, boy. So at least one of the horses had started crowding her, a typical power move. No doubt they all sensed that Lily wasn't the leader of the herd. She didn't understand that they'd take more and more liberties until some of them would become unmanageable and even dangerous, both to themselves and to her.

But she was genuinely fond of them after only two months, and he didn't want to mess with that. Homeless animals needed all the friends they could get, so he'd tread lightly. But she was going about this all wrong. If she didn't create some order and discipline soon, the situation could become unworkable.

Yeah, Nick could have been more forthcoming. Regan wondered why Nick hadn't put a stop to this laissez-faire attitude of hers. Regan planned to ask. In fact, he had a whole list of questions now that he'd been here.

Glancing around, he calculated how much time he'd need to rope each horse and do an exam. Even with her help, it would take too long, considering the other appointments he'd scheduled today. The horses might not be cooperative, either. Nick hadn't been to Peaceful Kingdom since early May, so no telling how they'd react to being examined after a month of doing as they pleased. "Maybe I should come back during their dinnertime, after all."

"That really would be better. Tell you what. If you'll do that, I'll feed you supper."

"That's really not necessary." He'd bet the keys to his truck that she was a vegetarian, maybe even vegan.

"I know, but it would make me feel better about inconveniencing you. Please say you'll stay for dinner."

"I wouldn't want to put you to any extra trouble on my account." Some people could make vegetables taste yummy and others couldn't. The minute he'd left home he'd reverted to being a carnivore, and so had his brothers and sisters. Even his parents weren't as strict these days, especially when they hung out at the Last Chance Ranch.

She grinned at him. "You think I'm going to serve you sprouts and tofu, don't you?"

Apparently she was good at reading expressions and had figured out why he was hesitating. "Are you?"

"Nope. I make a veggie lasagna that's out of this world. My parents love it, and they're dyed-in-the-wool carnivores."

"Real cheese?"

"Absolutely. I haven't hitched my wagon to the vegan concept yet. I still might some day, but I do love my cheese and ice cream."

She really was adorable. Had he been looking for adorable…but he wasn't. A mere six months ago he'd been kicked in the teeth, romantically speaking, and that had left a mark. "Then I accept. What time?"

"I feed the horses around five."

"I'll be here a little after five, then. It'll be much easier to examine them when they're each in a separate stall."

"Uh, they won't *all* be in separate stalls. About half won't, actually."

"Why not?"

"I have twelve stalls and twenty-one horses, so most of them double up."

Regan looked more closely at the pink-and-turquoise barn. Judging from the size of it, those twelve stalls wouldn't be oversized. "So you have a space problem?"

"I'm afraid I do." She gazed at him with those soulful blue eyes. "The thing is, I can't help but say yes."

That comment shouldn't have had a sexual connotation. But long after he'd driven away from the Peaceful Kingdom Horse Sanctuary, her words floated around in his traitorous brain.

She appeared to be a free spirit. That didn't necessarily mean she would embrace the concept of a no-strings affair, but it might. The thought created a pleasant ache in his groin. He hadn't felt that surge of desire in some time. Apparently he'd repressed it, because sure enough, thinking of sex brought up what had happened back in Virginia. Last Christmas Eve he'd found Drake Brewster, his best friend and business partner, in bed with Jeannette Trenton, his fiancée. That discovery had affected him more than anyone knew.

Jeannette had accused him of being cold-blooded because he'd refused to discuss it afterward. Instead, he'd handled the situation with surgical precision. Within a week he'd moved out of their shared condo, ended their engagement, sold his share of the veterinary practice to Brewster and relocated from Virginia to Jackson Hole, where Nick Chance had welcomed him into his practice. The move had been a no-brainer. He couldn't continue to work with Brewster after what the guy had done, and the previous summer Nick had mentioned needing a partner in his clinic.

Even more compelling was the prospect of being surrounded by family while he put his life back together. Nearly twenty years ago his folks had spent several months in Jackson Hole. His older sister Morgan had loved the place so much she'd vowed to return. When she finally made good on that promise to herself, she'd met and married Gabe Chance. Thus had begun the growing connection between the Chance family and the O'Connelli brood.

Next, Regan's twin sister, Tyler, had married into the Chance extended family. She was happily hitched to Alex Keller, brother of Jack Chance's wife, Josie. And most recently, eighteen-year-old Cassidy, youngest of the O'Connelli siblings, had apprenticed as the ranch housekeeper.

Sarah, the Chance family matriarch, had insisted that Regan stay at the Last Chance until he'd decided whether to live in town or buy some acreage. Six months later he was still there soaking up the ambiance. He'd never lived in a place that felt more like home, and he craved that sense of permanence.

For half a year he'd managed to convince himself that he'd moved past that fateful Christmas Eve when two people he'd trusted had betrayed him. He hadn't dated, but that seemed natural under the circumstances. Lily was the first woman he'd met who interested him, which was ironic. All the evidence suggested her philosophy of life was exactly like his parents' and the complete opposite of his.

But did that matter? He wasn't ready for anything serious. As for Lily, if she was the least bit like his parents, she'd grow bored with the horse sanctuary eventually and search for a new challenge somewhere else, so she wouldn't be around long.

But while she was, maybe they could hang out together. During their conversation she'd slipped in a comment about a potential wife or a girlfriend. Sometimes that meant a woman was trying to find out that information for her own reasons.

He'd know soon enough. She didn't strike him as a woman who was into mind games. No, she seemed forthright, playful and creative. Instead of wincing at her paint job, he should rejoice, because it told him that she enjoyed having fun. It had been so damned long since he'd had fun.

2

LILY STOOD BY the gate and waved as Regan drove away. She continued to watch until the plume of dust kicked up by his truck's tires disappeared. Long after he was gone, she stayed where she was, lost in thought. Regan O'Connelli was a pleasant surprise, even if he had informed her that she needed to change how she was running the sanctuary.

He'd meant it in a helpful way, though, and he might have a point. Nick had hinted at the same thing, but she'd been so convinced the horses deserved spoiling that she hadn't paid much attention. Besides, he was Nick, someone she'd known since she was a precocious whiz kid and he was one of her parents' favorite students in high school. He behaved toward her like the big brother she'd never had, and she expected him to dispense advice, most of which she would ignore.

In this case, maybe she shouldn't have ignored it. She was a little embarrassed by how quickly her situation was getting out of hand. Each day she worked to be more efficient, but then a new horse would arrive and she'd struggle to get all her chores done.

She probably shouldn't accept any more horses, but how could she turn them away if they had nowhere to go? She needed to find homes for some of them, but she hadn't figured out the adoption part of the plan. Come to think of it, the Turners hadn't mentioned it, either. They'd both been a little absent-minded during the transfer of ownership, and she hadn't thought to ask.

Regan might have some suggestions. She smiled to herself. The guy was hot. As she finally admitted that she'd noticed that, she laughed. His hotness was the real reason she was standing here dreamy-eyed over her new vet.

He was one juicy dude, in a Johnny Depp kind of way. That comparison couldn't be confirmed until she'd found out whether he had dark eyes, and he'd kept his bad-boy shades on the entire time, darn it. What a great idea, inviting him to dinner so he'd be around after the sun went down.

Maybe he'd kept the shades on because he had sensitive eyes, but she wondered if something else was going on with him. Sunglasses could also provide emotional protection. She'd always been super conscious of people's emotions, and after hanging out with rescue animals, she picked up on their moods, too. Understandably, many of the horses had trust issues, and she'd felt the same vibe coming from Regan.

Buck plodded over and nudged her from behind, so she turned to give the sway-backed horse some neck scratches. "I could be wrong, Buck, old boy, but I think that guy might need to be rescued as much as the rest of you around here."

The horse bobbed his head, and Lily smiled. "Thanks for validating my hypothesis." She patted his neck and reached for the cell phone in her back pocket. "Let's see if Dr. Chance agrees with me." She scrolled through her contacts and called Nick.

He answered on the second ring. "How'd it go with Regan?"

"Fine. You busy?" Holding the phone to her ear, she set off in search of the two pigs. They were probably okay, but she wanted to make sure.

"Yeah, I'm an extremely busy and important man, but for you, I'm willing to postpone my critical work for a few minutes."

"You are so full of it. I'm convinced you passed my mom's class purely on your ability to BS."

"I might've. But I aced your dad's science class with a minimum of BS. Just ask him."

"Don't have to. You two have a mutual admiration society going on." She located the pigs wallowing in the large mud pit she'd dug a few days ago for Wilbur. Harley was going to fit right in. "I like Regan a lot, although he's already telling me I'm doing this horse thing wrong."

"What does he think you're doing wrong?"

"Letting the horses roam the property, for starters."

"Well, Regan prefers more order than that, but those six horses are pretty old. I don't think it'll hurt to let them have some freedom in their golden years."

"I, um, have more than six, now. And they're not all in their golden years."

"Oh? How many do you have?"

"Twenty-one."

"Good golly, Miss Molly! What did you do, adver-tise?"

"Not exactly, but I've talked to people when I go

into town. Oh, and I redesigned the website and made sure it came up on all the search engines. It's a kick-ass site, if I do say so."

"I'll bet."

"I guess the word got out that I was here and had room for more horses."

"I'm sure it did." Nick was quiet for a bit. "Lily, you don't have room in your current barn to keep twenty-one horses forever. You'll have to renovate that barn and add more stalls."

"What do you mean, *forever?* Won't people come and adopt some of them?"

"Not usually. You have a sanctuary, which means you take in animals that are too sick or old to be ridden anymore and you keep them until they die."

"Oh." How embarrassing. She hadn't understood the basic premise of the project she'd taken on. "What do you call a place where you adopt out some of the horses?"

"I'm not sure. Maybe an equine rescue facility. But not a sanctuary."

Lily swallowed. "Well, that's what I need this to be, then, an equine rescue facility, at least for the animals I've taken in since I arrived. They're not old and ready to die. People didn't want them, so I accepted them. I thought that was what I was supposed to do."

"It's okay. No harm done. But you can't ever adopt out those original six. They're there for the duration."

"I did figure that, but the barn holds twelve, and I thought it was a shame for the other stalls to go to waste." Still, she felt like an idiot.

"Don't worry. You can sort this out. What's your plan for the adoption process?"

"Um...I'm working on it." She hated to admit that no plan existed yet, but it couldn't be that hard. She'd had no trouble finding people who wanted to get rid of horses, so now she needed to find the other half, the ones who wanted horses. "I should also probably mention the chickens."

"What chickens?"

"Rescue chickens. I have nine of them."

"How the hell did that happen?"

"I said yes to one person, and before you know it, I had nine."

Nick sighed. "Do you know anything about chickens?"

"Enough to know I don't want a rooster!"

"That's a start." He didn't sound quite as confident now.

"I'm okay with the chickens, Nick. Mom and Dad had some a few years back, so they're helping me figure it out. I also have two potbellied pigs. You'd be amazed how much info Google can dig up on potbellied pigs."

"Good Lord. You know, Lily, you don't need to accept every animal that shows up at your gate."

"That's what I tell myself, but I worry what will happen to them if I don't."

He sighed. "Yeah, that's a problem when you get into the rescue business, but here's the deal. You have accepted twenty-one horses, nine chickens and two pigs. I'm sure they keep you busy."

"They do." She had almost no downtime these days. She hadn't played a video game in weeks, and her meditation practice was shot, but so far she'd kept up with the critters.

"Think about the animals you already have before

you take in any more, okay? You owe those animals your best, and the larger your numbers, the less you'll be able to give them your best."

"I could hire help."

"You could, but you're still limited to the space you have. When winter comes, you'll want to keep the horses in the barn most of the time, and that barn's not big enough for twenty-one horses."

"I could add on or build another one, like you said."

"But where does it stop? Are you planning to buy more land and just keep building barns? How big an operation do you want?"

Lily took a deep breath. "I don't want a big operation. I love this property just the size it is. It suits me, and the idea of employees gives me hives. I'd have to fill out IRS stuff and get them health insurance and learn how to be the boss of them."

"If you don't want to expand, you know what you have to do."

"Right. Turn away any incoming horses until I adopt some out and make room." Her stomach hurt. How could she refuse to take a homeless animal? That would kill her.

"Good. And about letting them roam everywhere, you might want to—"

"I know. Regan pointed out that they won't be adoptable unless they have good manners, and some of the younger ones aren't all that well behaved. A couple of them act like they want to fight with each other. I probably need to stop letting them run loose."

"Yes, you do. They need to adapt to normal restrictions or nobody will want them. A well-trained horse is much easier to adopt out."

For the first time since she'd moved onto the property, she felt uncertain that she'd done the right thing. She should have asked more questions instead of blithely leaping into something because it had sounded cozy. She'd liked the idea of doing something good for the planet. On the surface a horse sanctuary had seemed romantic and not particularly complicated. She'd loved the name of the place. Someone with the last name of King should have a kingdom, right?

If she'd understood that she was only supposed to take care of animals on their last legs, she might not have bought Peaceful Kingdom. Sure, somebody needed to do it, but she didn't have the temperament. She'd be bored out of her tree, which might have been why she'd encouraged the locals to bring in more horses and liven things up.

Now she had to whip these newly acquired equines into shape fast and find them good homes so she could keep taking in the needy ones that would be lining up outside her gate with woeful expressions in their beautiful big eyes. The word was spreading, and in tough economic times, many people couldn't afford to keep the horse they'd bought in a burst of optimism. That was the story most everyone had given her when they'd arrived at her gate.

Her next admission was so hard to make. "Nick, I don't know how to train a horse."

"That's no problem. You're a smart person. I'll talk to Regan and see if he can help you. I'll help you, too, when I can, but Regan has a little more free time than I do. He'll probably agree. He's a good guy."

She latched on to this new topic with relief. "Speaking of Regan, what's his deal, Nick?"

He hesitated. "What do you mean?"

"You don't have to tell me if you shouldn't, but I get the impression something bad happened to him recently. He seems…wounded."

"What made you think that?"

"He didn't take off his shades."

"He examined all the horses with his sunglasses on? That doesn't sound like Regan. He's usually super professional."

"He didn't examine the horses. He's coming back tonight when they're all in the barn." As she said it, she realized that expecting him to make a second trip really was ridiculous. Both Regan and Nick were right. She had too many horses and no control of them. That had to change.

"So what did he do while he was out there, if he didn't examine the horses?"

"Helped carry the pig crate in here, and then we talked for a little while. That's when he mentioned that I might be headed down the wrong road here at Peaceful Kingdom." She gazed at the porch rail Sally was currently chewing on. Then she walked over and gave the mare a swat on the rump. Sally barely flinched and kept chewing. "So am I right? Is Regan hiding behind those shades?"

"I never thought about it before. He does wear them a lot. Most of us are fine with using our hats to shade our eyes. Sunglasses just get in the way."

"He had the hat on, too. Double protection. I just thought, if he's going to be advising me, I should know if there are certain subjects to avoid. I don't want to stumble over a psychological land mine." That was absolutely true. Regan was beginning to look like her savior, and she didn't want to tick him off accidentally. She'd already created a problem for herself with the horses. She couldn't afford to make the situation worse by alienating someone who could help.

Nick was silent for a moment. "I suppose it might be good for you to know. Everyone at the ranch does. But you can't tell him I told you."

"I won't."

"Okay, last Christmas Eve, he found his fiancée with his best friend."

Lily's chest tightened. "In bed?"

"Yeah."

"Damn." Now she wished she hadn't been right about Regan's vulnerability. "No wonder he's wearing shades. I would, too. I've never had a fiancé, but I can imagine that would feel pretty awful, especially if it was with your best friend."

"Don't let on that you know, although maybe it *is* better that you do know. We all feel protective of him. He'll be fine, but I don't think he's totally over it yet."

"How could he be? Poor thing. It's only been six months." That meant he was off-limits to her, though. She had no interest in being some gorgeous guy's rebound girl, even if she did want to soothe his wounded heart. She'd tried that once and it hadn't turned out well. The rebound girl served a purpose, she'd discovered, but once that purpose was gone, so was the guy, which left the girl feeling used. "Anyway, thanks for filling me in."

"You bet. Gotta go. He just walked into the office."

"Okay. 'Bye." She disconnected the call. What a

shame about the fiancée and the best friend. Good to know, she supposed, and she owed Nick big-time for telling her. But her Johnny Depp fantasy had officially bitten the dust.

TECHNICALLY, REGAN SHOULD be frustrated as hell with the situation in Lily's pink-and-turquoise barn. The quarters were cramped and the horses tested him continually. He'd countered every attempt to gain control with a stern word and a flick of the lead rope. So far that had kept any misbehaving animals in line.

But he'd had to remain vigilant. He should hate being here in this chaotic environment, except that it also contained Lily, who watched his every move. She asked excellent questions and took detailed notes on her phone, which he found endearing.

Earlier today he'd talked with Nick, who'd clarified the sanctuary-versus-rescue mix-up. Regan hadn't been clear on the terms until then, either, but now he understood a little better how Lily had landed in this mess. Nick had wanted to know if Regan could spare some time to help her. Damn straight. Catching a glimpse of her bright hair and ready smile made his heart lift. He wouldn't mind coming out here on a regular basis. It would be no sacrifice at all.

At last they were done, and she turned to him. "Should I keep them inside tonight so they'll start getting used to the idea?"

"It's pretty crowded. How about if we split them up and lead a few into the corral, instead?"

"That's a good plan, except the gate's broken. Mr. Turner told me he'd meant to fix it, but his arthritis was so bad he never did."

"How broken is it?"

"It's coming off the hinges. I decided not to worry about the corral, so I don't know if it could be easily fixed or whether I need a whole new gate."

"Let's leave them in here for now and take a look."

She nodded. "Sounds like a plan."

As he walked with her toward the corral, he noticed that the orange-red glow of the sunset matched the color of her hair. Nice. But the setting sun also brought out the unusual colors of the ranch buildings, prompting him to ask the question that had been nagging him for hours. "Why did you paint the buildings such…unusual colors?" He was proud of himself for substituting *unusual* for *god-awful*.

"Several reasons. First of all, these colors make me happy. I also like doing the unexpected thing to keep me from being bored. Nobody in this area has a pink-and-turquoise barn or an orange-and-green ranch house."

"That would be true."

"Besides that, I wanted to make sure people could find the place, and you have to admit that the colors make it stand out."

"Also true."

"But you don't care for them."

He smiled to soften his response. "No, not really."

"I'm not surprised." She said it in a conversational tone, as if his answer hadn't fazed him in the least. Apparently she'd been expecting him to turn thumbs down.

Damn, now he wanted to know why. Did she think he was too boring to appreciate her creativity? Had he come across as someone with no imagination who always did what others expected? That was a stodgy image he wasn't crazy about, but it might be accurate.

In any case, he didn't have to worry about hurting her feelings. Obviously she didn't need his approval to feel good about her choice of paint, and she'd accepted his comment without taking it personally.

Her attitude made him look at the colors differently. Why shouldn't she be surrounded by colors that made her happy? It was her place, after all, and a little paint wasn't going to hurt anything. If it shook people out of a rut—stodgy people like him, for example—that could be a good thing. And she was right about making the place easy to find.

"I may have made the place too accessible, though." She paused and turned toward him. "The truth is, Regan, I blundered into this without the necessary skill set, and that's embarrassing. I don't have the foggiest idea what I'm doing, other than I want to help homeless horses."

"That's a good start." Her honesty touched him. "Don't be too hard on yourself. If everybody waited until they had the necessary skills before they started something, we'd still be living in caves."

"What a nice thing to say." Gratitude shone in her eyes. "Nick said he'd ask you about helping me. Did he?"

"Yeah."

"Will you? Do you have time?"

He didn't even have to think about it. "I'll make the time."

Her expression brightened. "Thank you, Regan."

As he gazed into her eyes, the pressure that had constricted his chest for months began to ease. Exercise hadn't eliminated it, and neither had booze. But granting one heartfelt request from Lily King made him feel lighter than air.

He should be thanking *her*. He wanted to stick around and see if she had any other miracle cures up her tie-dyed sleeve. An emotion washed through him, one he couldn't immediately identify. Then he figured it out. For the first time in ages, he was happy.

3

LONG BEFORE THE sun went down, Lily found out that Regan had brown eyes. He'd taken off both hat and sunglasses while he examined the horses. Whenever he'd glanced up to discuss something with her, she'd looked into the velvet depths of those brown eyes and wished like hell he hadn't been dumped so recently.

Later on, he'd delivered a line guaranteed to make a woman swoon—*I'll make the time.* He'd compounded the effect of that by demonstrating that he knew exactly how to fix her broken gate. A man with multiple skills—now that was sexy. She was handy with a paintbrush, but she hadn't taught herself to use the array of tools Mr. Turner had left her.

She would learn eventually, but watching Regan took away a big chunk of her incentive, especially after he rolled up his sleeves to reveal the play of muscles as he worked. She'd have no trouble being into Regan O'Connelli. As she held the gate steady while he reattached the hinges, she wondered what sort of idiot would cheat on a guy who seemed so special.

Then she chastised herself for making a snap judgment. She didn't know the whole story, only the version presented by Nick, who was clearly biased in Regan's favor. There might have been extenuating circumstances. If she kept her distance as she planned, she'd never know.

Maintaining that distance would be more of a challenge than she'd counted on, though. He was definitely a wounded man in need of comfort. She'd sensed it when they'd met, but at that point his shields had been firmly in place.

Apparently his thinking had changed in the intervening hours, because now he was lowering those shields. She heard it in his voice, as brisk efficiency was replaced with mellow goodwill. His body language was more open, too. No more crossed arms or clenched jaw when he talked with her.

But mostly she saw it in his eyes. They flashed with interest now instead of wariness. Fortunately she could resist those flashes of interest. What sucked her in were the brief moments when she glimpsed sadness and pain in those beautiful brown depths.

If a more powerful aphrodisiac existed, she didn't know what it was. Responding to it was a huge mistake, as she'd long ago discovered to her sorrow. But he was a gorgeous man with a broken heart, and what woman wouldn't yearn to help him heal?

This woman. Taking a deep breath, she tightened her resolve to keep Regan at arm's length. She'd learned her lesson, right?

"That should do it." He swung the gate back and forth a couple of times and made sure the latch fastened securely.

"Thank you." She gave him a smile and vowed to get

comfortable with repair work. The less she needed from Regan, the easier it would be for her to resist temptation.

"Let's gather a few horses." He started back toward the barn.

She fell into step beside him. "I promise that's the only handyman chore I'll ask of you."

He shrugged. "It's no problem. I'm used to repairing things."

"Maybe so, but if I'm going to run this place, I should make friends with hand tools."

"I would agree with that. Shouldn't be too tough for you to learn. Nick said you were a smart cookie."

"He did?" That pleased her. "Just out of curiosity, what else did he tell you about me?"

"That you created a video game that's paying for all this." He swept an arm to encompass the property. "That's impressive."

"I guess. But I'm not sure it makes much of a contribution to the betterment of humanity."

"Why, is it violent?"

"God, no. I'm not into that kind of game. It's about elves and magic. There is a dragon, but he's more comic relief than scary. If you give him enough treats, which are increasingly hard to come by as the game goes on, he doesn't cause problems."

"Sounds like fun. Maybe we could play it some—" He was interrupted by the high-pitched scream of a horse followed by several loud thuds. "Shit." He took off at a run toward the barn.

Lily ran after him, her heart thumping. Two of the geldings, a big roan named Strawberry and a palomino named Rex, had never cared for each other. She'd put them in different stalls with horses they seemed to like, so it couldn't be them fighting, could it?

Regan beat her into the barn and grabbed a lead rope from a peg on the wall. He strode quickly to Rex's stall. The palomino bared his teeth at a young gelding named Sandy who had never caused a single problem since he'd been brought in two weeks earlier. Sandy cowered against the far wall, eyes rolling with fright. At least he didn't seem to be bleeding anywhere.

"Hey!" Regan's voice rang out. Opening the stall door, he walked in, the tail end of the lead rope flicking back and forth in front of him. "Back off!" He edged into position and snapped the rope in front of Rex's face.

Lily held her breath. A rope didn't seem like much protection against a riled-up horse, but it was working some kind of magic on Rex. The palomino backed up a step, and then another.

Regan followed and kept that rope dancing in front of Rex's nose. Then, in one quick move, he clipped the front end of the rope to Rex's halter and pulled the horse's head down. "Enough of that, mister. We're going for a walk."

As Regan led Rex from the stall, Lily stood to one side and gave them room. "What can I do to help?"

"Latch the door after me, then walk ahead and open the corral. We'll put him in there to cool off."

"Right." She wanted to comfort Sandy, but that would have to be put on hold. After securing the stall door, she waited until Regan and Rex had left the barn before scooting around them and heading for the corral.

As she passed Regan, she heard him talking to Rex in a low, soothing voice. She didn't like to think about what would have happened if Regan hadn't been here.

Of course, if he hadn't, the horses would have been free to leave the barn once they'd eaten, so this confrontation wouldn't have happened in the first place. Rex was used to eating and leaving for a far corner of the property. He usually took several horses with him. This time he'd been kept inside while all twenty-one animals were examined, and then the humans had disappeared without letting him loose. Apparently that hadn't sat well with him.

After opening the gate, which moved smoothly on its hinges, Lily watched Regan approach with the horse. Rex ambled along as if he had nothing on his mind besides walking docilely toward the corral. He didn't crowd Regan the way Buck tended to crowd Lily, but he didn't hang back, either. Instead he behaved like the well-trained horse he might be if someone like Regan was in charge.

Speaking of the bodacious Dr. O'Connelli, he looked mighty fine coming toward her with that loose-hipped stride that emphasized the fit of his jeans. Each time he put a booted foot forward, the denim stretched across his thighs. She couldn't help but notice that. Any woman worth her salt would agree that he was one good-looking dude.

Fate wasn't being kind to her. She'd broken up with her steady boyfriend last fall. He hadn't approved of her plan to leave her job with a tech company in Silicon Valley and find a worthwhile charity to support in her hometown. Instead he'd been after her to create another moneymaking game and buy a Porsche or some other stupid luxury car.

She didn't miss Alfred, who'd turned out to have a completely different value system from hers. But she sure missed the sex. Until Regan had shown up outside her gate, she hadn't realized how much she missed it.

Unbeknownst to him, probably, he was a walking invitation to partake of those pleasures. Much as she strove to be nonjudgmental about his ex, the thought continued to surface—the woman was an idiot. Regan was brave, resourceful and breathtakingly handsome. Maybe he left dirty socks on the floor and the toilet seat up. Lily could forgive even those sins for a chance to jump his bones. His off-limits bones. Damn.

He continued to talk to Rex as he led the gelding into the corral. Then he removed the lead rope and gave Rex a slap on the rump. The palomino took off, and Regan came to stand beside her, coiling the lead rope. "We're going to have to watch that one."

"I can see that." Lily closed and latched the gate. "You scared me to death walking into the stall with only a rope."

"It usually works. I was ready to back out again if he'd turned on me. I'm no hero when it comes to dealing with a two-thousand-pound animal in a bad mood."

"Could've fooled me."

He gave her a lopsided grin. "Aw, shucks, ma'am. T'weren't nothin'."

Please don't be charming. She was having enough trouble keeping her libido in check. "Why does flicking a rope work?"

"Most horses hate having something flicked in their face, and the more you do it, the more they back away from it. It's a great way to get them to move without hurting them."

Lily thought of her futile attempt to coax Sally away from the porch railing this morning. "What if you don't have a rope handy? I can't picture myself carrying one around all the time."

"Ideally you would have a lead rope clipped to their halter when you're working with them."

"Okay, but what about the times I'm not working with them and they're…"

"Loose?"

She flushed. "I know. They shouldn't be loose, but there's no way I can adopt out six or seven horses in the next few days, and I don't like the idea of keeping them cooped up in the barn all the time. Even the corral is confining."

"You're right. You should only be using the corral for training. You could fence off a couple of acres so they have some room to run around, and then they won't be chewing on your house or pooping in your front yard."

She stared at him. "That's *brilliant*. Why didn't I think of that?"

"You didn't want to restrict their freedom."

She had said that, but coming from him, especially after the scare they'd just had, it sounded naive. "I've revised my opinion. But getting someone out here to construct the fence will take a while. What should I do in the meantime? Walk around carrying a rope?"

"You could carry a leather quirt and stick it in your back pocket."

"So I could hit them with it? I don't want to do that."

"Chances are you wouldn't have to touch them. You'd just wave it in their face like you would a rope."

"I'll think about it." She couldn't imagine walking around with a quirt stuck in her back pocket, either. She'd probably lose the darn thing. "Couldn't I just clap my hands and achieve the same thing?"

"Not really."

She sighed and glanced over at Rex, who was prancing around with his tail in the air, as if he owned that little circle. "Rex seems to like this setup just fine. He's king of the corral."

"So that's his name? I couldn't remember, but it fits him. He wants to rule any situation he's in, I'll bet. Did the people who brought him in say anything about his personality?"

Lily thought back to the young woman who'd left Rex at the sanctuary. "She said he was too much horse for her. She was small, so I thought that's what she meant. Rex came here shortly after I took over, so at first he only had the old horses to deal with."

"And he could boss them around."

"They didn't seem to mind. Strawberry, the big roan, was the first horse to challenge Rex, but after they did a little snorting and pawing, they stayed away from each other. I kept Rex in a stall by himself until recently. I thought he'd be okay with Sandy, who's not aggressive at all. And it worked out until tonight."

Regan nudged back the brim of his hat and glanced over at the barn. "I don't want to chance putting anyone else in the corral with Rex tonight. He might be fine, but he might not. I guess we have to turn them all loose again. It's what they're used to."

"And now I have a strategy to prevent Sally from trying to come in the house. I'll keep a rope handy."

"You know why she does that, right?"

"Sure. She thinks she's a dog. Or a person."

"No, she's trying to gain more control over you. Horses will push when they sense you're not in charge."

That made her laugh. "I think it's pretty obvious by now that I'm not in charge. Far from it, in fact."

"But you need to be," he said quietly.

"Boy, that sounded serious."

"It is serious. These are big animals, very strong animals. They're used to having a leader of the herd, and if you don't accept that role, one of them will take it. Rex may think he already has. Strawberry might decide to fight him for it. Losing control is dangerous to them and dangerous to you."

Her pulse rate picked up, and this time it had nothing to do with how beautiful his eyes were and how much she wanted to do him. "Regan, you're scaring me."

"Good. I mean to. You've been lucky so far. Most of the horses haven't been here very long, and at least six of them are too old to harm anyone. But you need to let them all know you're the boss, and very soon."

A shiver ran down her spine. "I don't have the skills to do that, yet. I'll need training as much as they do. And practice. I'll call somebody first thing in the morning about fencing in a couple of acres. Oh, wait, what's tomorrow?"

"Saturday."

She groaned. "Some fencing companies will be closed, and even if I find one that isn't, they probably won't be able to finish it up until the first part of next week."

"I could ask Nick if he could pull in a favor. The Chance name might help."

"Sure, okay." She combed her fingers through her hair while she thought through her options. "I'm not too proud to accept that. If you'll call him now, I'll let the horses out."

"Look, I'm sorry to be the bearer of bad news, but I'm worried about you."

"I know." She drew in a shaky breath. "I just never imagined that my good deed could turn into a life-threatening situation—for me or for the other horses. Call Nick. I'll be right back. Then we should feed the pigs and the chickens."

Turning, she walked toward the barn. Her rose-colored glasses were smashed to smithereens, and as she entered the overcrowded space, she could swear ominous music played in the background. The horses looked the same, though, and gazing into their liquid-brown eyes as she opened each stall door calmed her. She gave an extra pat to Sandy, who seemed to have recovered from his fright.

They all walked out of the barn in the same leisurely fashion they normally did. But she couldn't quite erase her mental image of Rex and Strawberry battling to the death for control of the herd. That wasn't going to happen, though. She had Regan on her side, and he knew his way around these animals, thank God.

At last she opened the stall where Sally stood with a chestnut gelding named Brown Sugar. The gelding meandered out, but Sally lingered as if hoping for a treat. That was Lily's fault. She'd often slipped the little mare pieces of carrot and apple.

"Sorry, girl. No treats on me, tonight." She stroked the horse's silky neck. "You aren't really trying to control me, are you? You just want to be good friends."

Sally butted her head against Lily's chest.

"See, that's what I thought. Come on. Everybody else has left the barn, so you might as well, too." She turned and started down the wooden aisle.

Sally followed, but she didn't stay slightly back the way Rex had when Regan had led him toward the corral. She came right up to Lily, her nose often bumping Lily's arm. Lily moved over, and Sally moved with her.

As an experiment, Lily kept moving to the right each time Sally crowded her. Pretty soon she was out of room. She turned to face the mare. "Are you *herding* me?"

Sally's big brown eyes gave nothing away.

But Lily had her answer. Sally was in charge, and Lily wasn't. She had no rope or quirt, so she untied the tails of the shirt knotted at her waist and flapped those in front of the mare's face. "Back off, sweetheart!"

Sally's head jerked up and she took a couple of steps backward.

"Yep, that's what I'm talking about! Give me some room!" Lily flapped her shirt a few more times, and Sally retreated again. "Huh. Amazing."

She'd managed to intimidate Sally a little bit, but she had no illusions that she'd get the same respect from Rex or Strawberry. For that matter, most of the new arrivals might not pay any attention to her efforts. She had a lot to learn, and not much time to learn it. Knotting her shirt at her waist once again, she walked out of the barn into the soft twilight, followed at a respectful distance by Sally.

Regan, looking better with every minute that passed, came to meet her.

She was excited to share her small triumph with him. "Hey, you may not believe it, but I backed Sally off by undoing my shirt and flapping the ends in her face."

"Excellent!" He smiled. "Creative solution. Maybe you don't need a rope after all."

"Yeah, I do. I don't think my shirttails will make much of an impression on Rex."

"Maybe not. Anyway, I talked to Nick, and he'll do what he can, but summer is the worst time to get a crew ASAP. Busiest time of the year for fence companies because it's when they repair winter storm damage."

"Not surprising." But it wasn't the news she'd hoped to hear.

"He said he'd offer to send out some of the ranch hands, but there's a special riding event in Cheyenne this weekend, so he's short a few guys as it is. He can get right on it Monday morning, though."

"So I'm on my own with twenty-one horses who could decide to revolt at any moment."

"No, they won't." Concern shadowed his eyes. "I didn't mean to scare you *that* much. I just wanted to make a point."

"You made it, and I'm not sure how well I'm going to sleep tonight."

"You'll be fine. You can call me if there's a problem. I don't have any appointments tomorrow, so I can come out and check on you. I can do the same thing on Sunday."

"I have a better idea." It wasn't a wise idea, but desperate times called for desperate measures. "Don't take this the wrong way, but would you be willing to spend the weekend with me?"

4

REGAN GULPED. "EXCUSE ME?" His heart galloped out of control. Surely she hadn't suggested what he thought she had. He suddenly had trouble breathing.

Lily, she of the sunset-red hair and sky-blue eyes, seemed completely calm, though. "To be clear, that wasn't a proposition."

"Of course it wasn't. We barely know each other. I didn't think that at all." The hell he hadn't. Stupid of him, but he'd immediately created a cozy scenario for the two of them. Apparently his subconscious had been building a whole fantasy on her *I can't help saying yes* comment.

"The ranch house has a guest room. My mom insisted I should have one in case any of my friends from Berkeley show up. I realize this is a terrible imposition, but after Rex's little stunt, I'm worried about being alone here."

That was mostly his fault. "It's highly unlikely you'll have a problem." But what if she did? What if he drove away from here and something happened? What if she tried to break up a fight and got hurt in the process? He'd never forgive himself.

"I may be overreacting, but I've been jerked out of my blissful ignorance and there's no going back to it. I now understand the potential danger here. You know horses, and you're a vet who could deal with an injury if we were unlucky enough to have one. I'd consider it a huge favor if you'd do this."

He struggled to get his bearings. "Well, I—"

"This is spur of the moment, so if you're willing to stay, you might want to go home and get some things. Where are you living, by the way? I never thought to ask."

"At the Last Chance. Sarah gave me a room there in January, and I haven't decided whether to buy property, so I'm still at the ranch." He worked hard to seem as cool as she was about this discussion. She needed him to be there in case she had a problem with the horses. After the picture he'd painted, he couldn't blame her. Because he'd contributed to her nervousness, he should agree to her plan. It was the gentlemanly thing to do.

Unfortunately, the thought of spending the night in her house continued to suggest ungentlemanly ideas. That didn't mean he would act on them, though. He might have considered a relationship down the road, but getting sexually involved with her when they'd met only this morning would be insane. He'd never operated that way, and he wouldn't start now.

That didn't take into account how *she* operated, however. He considered the psychedelic colors of the buildings and her belief in letting all creatures run free. That could add up to a woman who didn't have rigid rules of behavior when it came to sex. But apparently he did.

Could he change those rules given the right circumstances? Yes.

"I can feed the pigs and the chickens if you want to
head back to the ranch and pick up a few things. That's
if you're even willing to consider doing this."

"So it would ease your mind if I did?" Dumb question. He knew it would because she'd already said so.
And he knew his answer was yes.

He was stalling because he hadn't decided whether
to drive back to the ranch for a change of clothes and
a shaving kit. That could be problematic if he ran into
someone who asked questions. No one kept close track
of him there, so if he didn't show up, they might assume he was out on a call that lasted into the night.
That would be sort of true. He'd like to keep their arrangement on the down-low for now.

"It would greatly ease my mind." She looked up at
him. "Please say you'll stay. I'm a decent hostess."

His breath caught. She was pleading with him to
do this because she was frightened, not because she
wanted him in her bed. Thoughts of sex were far from
her mind, and they should be far from his, too. They
would be. He'd stay for a couple of nights and guarantee
her a peaceful weekend free of worries about her horses.

Maybe in a few weeks the situation would resolve
itself and he could ask her out. But only a jerk would
take advantage of a woman's fears—fears he'd helped
foster. He was better than that.

"I'll stay," he said. "I don't need to go back to the
ranch for anything. If you have a spare toothbrush, I
can manage." And if he didn't go back to the ranch, he
wouldn't be tempted to grab the box of condoms that

he'd discovered in the upstairs bathroom. Even more reason to stay right here and be virtuous as hell.

"Thank you, Regan. You're a good guy."

He wasn't so sure about that, but he would do his damnedest to be a good guy for the next forty-eight hours. "Ready to feed the pigs and chickens?"

"Absolutely!" Her bright smile flashed.

Yeah, he could do this. The relief in her smile was all the reward he needed. If he hadn't believed every word of warning he'd spoken, he'd feel guilty about scaring her. But she needed to understand what she was up against. Chances were nothing would happen this weekend, but if it did, he'd be here to help.

Feeding the chickens, it turned out, was easy. He felt like Old MacDonald as he scattered seed over the ground. The pigs were a lot more work. First he and Lily had to chop up an ungodly amount of fresh vegetables. They stood side by side tossing cut-up veggies into two large bowls about the size needed for a batch of cookie dough. He'd never expected to have fun preparing a meal for pigs. Once again his happiness meter registered somewhere near the top of the scale.

He threw a handful of carrot chunks into the bowl. "I thought they ate kitchen scraps."

"Most people think so, but they won't get a balanced diet that way." Lily chopped with rhythmic precision as she talked. "I found all kinds of information online, and everyone says to feed vegetables loaded with vitamins if you want a happy, healthy pig. And you're not supposed to overfeed them or they'll get fat. Harley looks a little overweight to me. What do you think?"

"I didn't spend any time studying pigs, so I'm no expert." Regan started in on a head of cabbage. "But he's definitely chunkier than Wilbur."

"And from what I've researched, Wilbur's about right. I'll have to make sure Harley doesn't try to steal any of Wilbur's food."

Regan finished with the cabbage and moved on to a sack of potatoes. "What if someone wants to adopt these guys? How will you know they'll feed them right?"

"Excellent question. I've thought about it a lot today. I've considered having the adopters sign an agreement that they'll follow the guidelines I give them and read the information on keeping pigs as pets. But what if they don't? How will I know?"

"You won't, which is why they might need to provide references."

"I think so, too. That's still no guarantee, because they can give me names of people who will say whatever they're supposed to, but it makes the process more complicated. People who want to adopt a pig on impulse won't want to go through all that."

Regan picked up a bunch of golden beets. "At least these are adult pigs, so nobody can kid themselves about the amount of room they'll need."

"I've toyed with the idea of a home visit before I let the pig go."

"It will take lots of extra time to do that."

"I know." Lily topped off her bowl with some bib lettuce. "But after you filled me in about Harley's deal, where his mud hole was competing for space with folks enjoying a backyard barbecue, I think viewing the future living space would be good. The requirements for the pig have to come first."

"Because pigs can't speak for themselves."

"Exactly!" She turned to beam at him. "Most of those who bring me horses, pigs or chickens are ready to dump an inconvenient nuisance. They've never thought about how they play havoc with the lives of creatures who can't speak for themselves. Or how they've contributed to the problem, which I've certainly been guilty of with the horses. I'm determined to fix that."

Regan laid down his knife and turned toward her. "I owe you an apology."

"For what?" She glanced up at him. "You've been nothing but helpful and kind."

"Not really. I've implied that you don't know what you're doing, but at your core, you know exactly what you're doing. You respect the rights of creatures who can't speak our language. They may have their own language, but they can't speak ours—and many of us marginalize them. You don't, and that's…that's wonderful." He had the strongest urge to kiss her, which would be so inappropriate. Coming on the heels of his little speech, it would seem opportunistic.

"Wow. Thank you." She seemed taken aback. "Lately I've been thinking I don't belong in this place."

"Don't ever think that." He'd watch how he worded his suggestions from now on, because he didn't want to discourage her from sticking it out. This morning he'd figured she might leave as soon as she grew bored, an assumption based on how his parents might react in this situation. But listening to her now, he wasn't sure about that.

"I can't help it, Regan. I wasn't qualified to take over, although I didn't have sense enough to know it at the time. But there was no one else, which helped me make up my mind. Now that I realize what I'm up against,

I should probably advertise for someone more experienced to buy it and run it."

Damn. In trying to make a point, he'd been too hard on her. "I hope you don't do that. If I've made you insecure about being here, I'm deeply sorry. You may not understand the herd mentality of horses, but that can be learned. What you have, empathy for all animals, is far more important."

She swallowed. "That means a lot to me, Regan. I was feeling pretty much like a dweeb an hour ago, but… what you just said helps."

"I'm glad." He could drown in those blue eyes, and he dared not. She'd invited him here for the good of the horses and so she wouldn't make some terrible mistake that would cause them harm. The emotion he saw in her eyes was related to that, and not to a personal connection between them.

She gazed up at him, her expression soft. Yeah, he wanted to kiss her.

Then she broke eye contact, and the moment was gone. She cleared her throat. "Ready to feed Wilbur and Harley?"

Either he'd misinterpreted the way she'd been looking at him, or she didn't want to get romantically involved. Either way, he'd do well to cool his jets. He gestured toward the bowl he'd been filling. "Nothing else will fit in here, so I suppose the answer is yes."

"Then let's go."

Resolving to avoid any more dreamy-eyed moments, he walked with her out to the mud hole she'd dug behind the ranch house. Once again he marveled at how deep it was. She'd engaged in some serious digging because she'd wanted Wilbur to feel at home, and now Harley could enjoy the results of her labor, too.

Both pigs lay in happy abandon in the mud, but they perked up the minute Lily and Regan arrived with dinner. Regan set down Harley's bowl, careful to put it a distance away from Wilbur's. With squeals of delight, each pig waddled toward his respective dinner and buried his snout in the pile of veggies.

"They're cute." Regan surprised himself by saying that.

"I know. I've already bonded with Wilbur. I have about fifty pictures of him on my phone. I took some of Harley today. They both have the most adorable faces."

"I can't see much of their faces right now, but I like the way they wag their little tails when they're happy. I also expected it to smell bad out here, but it doesn't."

"I'm pretty fanatical about cleaning up after my animals. These pigs may wallow in the mud, but I don't want them to stink. That's gross."

Regan hadn't thought much about it before, but the stalls had been spotless, too. No wonder he'd felt muscles when he'd grabbed her arm. She must be shoveling a good part of the day. "Have you thought of hiring someone to help deal with cleanup?"

"Nick mentioned that, too. I kind of like not worrying about an employee. If push comes to shove, I might have to get someone, but I don't want to rush into it."

Regan nodded and turned his attention back to the pigs. "They sure are tearing into that food, especially Harley."

"From what I've read, they'll eat as much as you give them, and they'll allow themselves to get overweight. But in other ways they're very smart. Their IQ is—

wait, I don't need to tell you. You're a vet. You probably know all that."

"I've heard they're intelligent, but that's about all I know. Aren't they smarter than most dogs?"

"They are, and I like that they have brains. I might have to keep these two instead of finding new homes for them."

Regan opened his mouth to say that more pigs would be coming because the word was out. She'd have to make sure she didn't bond with the next one, and the one after that, or she'd be overrun with pigs. Then he closed his mouth again.

If she wanted to keep twenty pigs, it wasn't the same as twenty horses. When the fence crew finally arrived, she could decide if she wanted an enclosure for her current potbellied friends and those who were sure to come later.

"You're worried that I'm going to load up on pigs the way I loaded up on horses and get myself into more trouble, aren't you?"

"Nope."

She laughed. "Liar."

"I do think you'll get more pigs, though. The guy who brought Harley heard about you from the people who had Wilbur. I don't know if there's a potbellied-pig hotline, but I wouldn't be surprised."

"I'm sure there is. I've thought about joining a potbellied-pig chat group, but I haven't had time. Maybe once I reduce the number of horses, I can hook up with other people who have pigs. These guys fascinate me. They're so different from your average domestic animal."

"That's for sure."

"Some people let them in the house, but I'm not ready to—whoops. There goes Harley after Wilbur's food." Lily hurried over and blocked Harley's progress. He let out an ear-splitting scream of frustration and plowed past her, knocking her smack-dab into the mud hole.

Without thinking twice, Regan waded in after her.

"Forget about me!" she wailed. "Pick up Wilbur's food bowl!"

"To hell with Wilbur's food bowl." He extended his hand. "Grab hold."

Harley had shoved Wilbur aside and was eagerly crunching on the remainder of the smaller pig's food. "I guess it's too late to get the food, anyway," she said. "He might try to bite you."

"*Might?* Did you hear him? I don't think there's any doubt he'd bite me." Harley wasn't the least bit cute anymore, either. Lily, on the other hand, was very cute sitting in the mud, her face and clothes splattered with globs of the stuff. He had a sudden image of her as a teenager in an old T-shirt and jeans with the knees busted out. In fact, she didn't look much older than sixteen now.

But the water and mud had begun to soak through her shirt. Very soon she'd go from cute to voluptuous, and that wouldn't be a good thing for a guy trying to keep his mind off sex. He wiggled his fingers. "Come on. Let's get you outta there."

With a sigh of resignation, she reached for his hand. "I'm all muddy."

"Are you? I hadn't noticed."

"Smart-ass. The sad thing is, your boots and the bottom of your jeans are muddy, too."

"That's the breaks." She was slippery now, and he

had trouble getting a grip on her. "Better give me both hands so I don't drop you back in the water."

He pulled, and she came out with a giant sucking sound, and way faster than he'd expected. Before he could adjust for her trajectory, she'd slammed into his chest. Good thing he'd dug in his heels before starting this maneuver or they would have both gone down. Instead they were plastered together like sheets of wet newspaper. He wrapped his arms around her to steady himself and discovered he was enjoying it far too much.

"Sorry. Didn't mean to do that." She tried to extricate herself.

Thrown off balance by her movements, he wobbled. "Careful. I don't have the best of footing. We're teetering."

She stood still. "Yeah, no point in making this any worse than it already is." She lifted her chin and looked into his eyes. She must have seen something more than simple concern there, because her breath hitched. "How do you suggest we proceed?"

"With caution." His pulse rate skyrocketed. So she'd guessed that he wanted to kiss her, mud specks and all. If she didn't want him to, he'd see it in her expression—a slight frown, a subtle narrowing of her eyes.

But she wasn't doing either of those things. Instead her eyes widened and her pupils dilated. "I absolutely agree." She ran her tongue over her lips, not in a seductive way, but quickly, as if checking for mud in case he decided to follow through.

"About what?" He'd lost track of the conversation. All his attention was focused on her plump lips, which were shiny from her tongue.

"Caution. Proceeding with it."

"You want to proceed?"

"I do." Her eyes darkened to midnight blue and her gentle sigh was filled to the brim with surrender as her arms slid around his neck, depositing mud along the way.

As if he gave a damn. His body hummed with anticipation. "Me, too." Slowly he lowered his head and closed his eyes.

"Mistake, though."

He hovered near her mouth, hardly daring to breathe. Had she changed her mind at the last minute? "Why?"

"Tell you later." She brought his head down and made the connection.

And it was as electric as he'd imagined. His blood fizzed as it raced through his body and eventually settled in his groin. Her lips fit perfectly against his from the first moment of contact. It seemed his mouth had been created for kissing Lily, and vice versa.

He tried a different angle, just to test that theory. Still perfect, still high voltage. Since they were standing in water, it was a wonder they didn't short out. He couldn't speak for her, but he'd bet he was glowing. His skin was hot enough to send off sparks.

She moaned and pressed her body closer. She felt amazing in his arms—soft, wet and slippery. He'd never imagined doing it in the mud, but suddenly that seemed like the best idea in the world.

Then she snorted. Odd. Not the reaction he would have expected considering where this seemed to be heading.

He lifted his head and gazed into her flushed face. "Did you just laugh?"

She regarded him with passion-filled eyes. "That wasn't me."

"Then who—"

The snort came again as something bumped the back of his knees. A heavy splash sent water up the back of his legs.

She might not have been laughing before, but she was now. "Um, we have company."

Although it didn't matter which pig had interrupted the moment, Regan had his money on Harley. Whichever one had decided to take an after-dinner mud bath, they'd ruined what had been a very promising kiss. Well, except for Lily's comment that it was a mistake.

Regan had hoped to move right past that comment, but he had a feeling she'd want to explain it more fully now that they weren't in a lip-lock. He knew one thing for sure, though. He was no longer a fan of those pigs.

5

LILY AND REGAN took off their muddy boots on the stoop outside the back door, which led directly into the kitchen. Once they were both inside, she grabbed some paper towels so they could clean off their hands. "Stay there for a sec." She finished wiping her hands. "I'll be right back with a robe for you."

She left the kitchen, hurried away from him through the small dining room and down a short hallway to the master bedroom and bath. She didn't want to discuss their kiss until they'd dealt with the mud.

She needed to tell him why the kiss had been a mistake, and therein lay her dilemma. She'd promised Nick she wouldn't mention Regan's breakup. Yet the breakup was at the heart of why she and Regan shouldn't become involved.

A brief period of insanity in a mud hole didn't have to turn into a full-blown disaster if she played this right. She'd lost focus when she'd inadvertently ended up in his arms, but she could make that momentary slip right. To fix it permanently, though, she had to explain how she felt about catching a guy on the rebound. That meant unearthing the truth about his situation…somehow, without involving Nick in any way.

Snatching her white terry robe from the hook on the back of her bathroom door, she returned to the kitchen. "This won't fit very well," she said as she handed him the robe, "but at least it's not pink."

He took it gingerly, being careful not to let it brush up against his muddy clothes. "I'm afraid I'll bust out your shoulder seams."

"It's roomier than it looks. And it's all I have for you to wear while I wash and dry your stuff. Just try it. I think you'll be surprised."

The corner of his mouth quirked up. "This whole evening has been one big surprise. I can't wait to see what happens next."

She decided not to touch that line. "The guest room is through the living room and down the hall on your right. There's a bathroom down there, too, and it's stocked with towels and stuff."

"Because your mom insisted."

"Yep. Turns out you're my first guest."

"I'm honored." He gave her an assessing glance. "Listen, are we going to talk about…"

"Sure. Absolutely. But let's get cleaned up, first. The lasagna is almost done."

"I figured. It smells great."

"I'll meet you back here in a little while. You should find everything you need. My mom's thorough about such things."

He nodded. "I'll be fine. See you in a few." Dangling the robe several inches in front of his body, he left the kitchen.

She retreated to her own bathroom. Moments later

she stood under a hot shower and evaluated her predicament. She'd brought it on herself, every bit of it. Her decision to buy Peaceful Kingdom had caused her to add more horses, two pigs and nine chickens. And she'd let them all roam at will. As if she hadn't created a big enough mess, she'd begged Regan to spend the next couple of nights in her house.

She'd had some room to maneuver…until she'd kissed him. She couldn't even claim that was his fault. He'd given her every opportunity to back out, but once she'd been chest to chest with all that glorious male beauty, she hadn't been able to resist him.

She could have stopped him at the very last minute, but what had she done? Pulled his head down and kissed the living daylights out of him, that's what. She was not what anyone would call a clutch player.

So now she had to clean up this fuster-cluck. Sending him home wasn't a solution, because sure as the world, she'd have an emergency and he'd end up back here, anyway. She was sitting on a keg of dynamite in more ways than one. Even her pigs weren't behaving themselves. Until she could get someone to build some sturdy fences, she needed Regan around.

That would work out just ducky if she could keep her hands to herself. He wasn't a Don Juan type who was plotting a seduction. If she set the boundaries, he'd abide by them. But she'd kissed him as if boundaries meant nothing. How to explain why she didn't want to continue with an activity she'd so obviously enjoyed?

Only one strategy occurred to her. If she could loosen his tongue so that he'd tell her about the breakup, she could explain why she chose to stay away from rebound relationships. She could say she'd sensed he might be hurting but hadn't wanted to pry. He might buy that.

It wasn't the greatest plan in the world, but she couldn't think of anything better. She had both beer and wine chilling in the refrigerator. The trick would be getting him to drink it while she only sipped.

Her bathroom routine took longer than she would have liked, but she'd had to wash her hair, and that meant doing something with it afterward. Blowing it dry would take forever, so she gathered it into a loose, damp arrangement on top of her head.

Leaving makeup off was a no-brainer. She wasn't trying to be more alluring, for crying out loud. Some old underwear might keep her from getting frisky.

Oh, hell, whom was she kidding? She'd never been the type to fuss with her appearance. She was strictly WYSIWYG—What You See Is What You Get. But if she didn't look sexy, that might make a difference to Regan. She put on her most raggedy sweatpants and a faded sweatshirt from Berkeley.

One glance in the mirror convinced her she'd done an awesome job. Only a desperate man would want to hit that. Of course, if Regan had gone without for six months, he might be on the desperate side. That also should be a warning to stay clear. He might not be hot for her, specifically. Maybe any reasonably good-looking woman would do.

After shoving her feet into some ratty slippers that once had been blue but had faded to a mottled gray, she padded into the aromatic kitchen with her armload of muddy clothes. Regan was nowhere in sight, so she carried her bundle into the laundry room located right off the kitchen and loaded the filthy clothes and some soap into the washing machine. Technically they shouldn't all be washed together, but mud was a game changer, in her opinion. Once he arrived with his clothes, they'd do a load of mud laundry and call it good.

"Here's my stuff."

She turned, and much as she tried not to, she stared. No woman with a pulse would have done any different when faced with Regan O'Connelli in an undersize bathrobe. He stretched the shoulders of that white terry to the breaking point, and the lapels didn't quite meet, so a sliver of his chest, complete with enticing dark hair, peeked through the opening.

He'd belted the robe as tightly as possible. Because he had narrow hips, the overlap was more than adequate there. Good thing, if he'd included his briefs in that pile he'd brought her. Although, in the long run, whether he was covered up didn't matter much. She still knew he likely was naked under that robe. How had she failed to calculate the effect of that on her little plan?

She accepted the clothes and shoved them in the washer. If he had any loose change or important pieces of paper in his pockets, oh, well. She wasn't taking the time to check. Her primary goal was to get everything washed and back on his body. His muscled, golden-skinned, infinitely lickable body...

Dear Lord, she was done for. Turning away from the washer, she dusted her hands together. "There. That's done."

"Lily?"

"What?"

"You didn't turn it on."

No, I didn't, because I'm already turned on enough

for both me and the washer to operate at top speed.
"Thanks." She walked back and punched the button.

"You were right." He held out his arms. "This fits better than I thought it would."

"So it does." She spun on her heel, because if she looked at him for even one second longer, she'd grab the sash of that robe and have her way with him. "Let's eat."

"Sounds good. I'm starving." He followed her into the kitchen.

She could swear, even though he was a good ten feet away from her, she heard every breath he took. She imagined what it would be like to run her fingers through his still-damp hair, to lay her palm against his chest and feel his heart pumping hot blood through his veins. Despite the spicy aroma of baked lasagna, she could smell the soap-fresh scent of his skin, and the underlying musk of virile, almost-naked male.

Her plan for resisting him seemed flimsy at best, but she'd stick to it as well as she could. "Which would you like with dinner, wine or beer?"

"With lasagna? Wine, I guess."

"Wine it is, then!" She knew she sounded deranged. Grabbing two wineglasses out of the cupboard, she took the Chardonnay out of the fridge.

"Let me open it." He walked over to the counter. "Got a corkscrew somewhere?"

"You bet. Second drawer from the left." She snatched up a couple of pot holders and made a beeline for the oven, which put some distance between her and Mr. Yum-Yum. If she'd had anything else to cover his body besides the terry robe, she'd be hauling it out now. There was the Hawaiian muumuu her mother had brought her from a trip to Maui a few years ago. Regan probably wouldn't go for that.

She pulled the lasagna pan out of the oven and managed to set it on top of the stove without dropping it. That was a little miracle in itself, considering how her hands were shaking.

"Wine?"

"Oh!" She turned to find him right next to her, a glass of Chardonnay extended. "Sure. Thanks." She accepted the glass and promptly gulped down a third of it before she remembered that hadn't been the strategy. But Regan O'Connelli was standing in her kitchen, naked except for a bathrobe that could come open *at any moment.* How could she be expected to keep her cool under those circumstances?

"Can I set the table?"

"Good idea." And it would get him out of the kitchen for a little while. "Utensils are in the first drawer from the left. You're a terrific guest. Somebody must have trained you well." No telling why she'd been compelled to say *that,* except that she tended to babble when she was nervous.

"My ex. I think she'd memorized the etiquette books."

Lily went completely still. Damn. A clue. Without getting him sloshed, she'd managed to extract a significant clue. But she had to handle the information with great delicacy. "You have an ex?" She hoped her nose wouldn't grow for that whopper.

"Doesn't everybody?"

Beep. Wrong answer. She closed her eyes in frustration. "I suppose so. I have an ex-boyfriend. What sort of ex do you have?" She crossed her fingers.

"Ex-fiancée."

"Ah. Recent?" She held her breath.

"Since last Christmas."

"Ouch. Tough time to break up."

He walked back, leaned in the archway separating the kitchen from the dining room and sipped his wine. "Is there ever a good time?"

"Guess not." Her heart ached for him. Nobody should be betrayed at Christmas, when everyone else was laughing and partying and kissing under the mistletoe. But he hadn't said his ex had betrayed him, only that they'd broken up. Lily vowed to remember that she was supposed to know only what he'd told her and nothing more.

She had enough information to make her case against sleeping with a guy on the rebound. Once they got into a discussion about the kiss they'd shared while standing in the mud hole, she'd be ready with her argument. She'd apologize for surrendering to the moment.

Most women succumbed to a man's charms under a silver moon while surrounded by fragrant blossoms and serenaded by violins. She'd almost given it up in a mud puddle.

"How soon before we eat?"

She snapped out of her daydream. Men liked to eat. She'd been without a boyfriend since last fall, and she'd forgotten a few things about the male of the species. "Let's give it ten more minutes to cool and set. I'd suggest we have a seat in the living room, but I don't have any furniture in there yet."

"I noticed."

"I'll get some eventually. My parents gave me their

old dining room table and chairs, but they're not ready to replace their living room stuff."

He gazed at her, a question in his eyes.

"You probably wonder why I don't just go out and get my own."

"It crossed my mind. You must care about this place, since you spent a lot of time painting the outside of all the buildings."

"Because painting is fun! I would have painted inside, too, but then more horses arrived, along with the chickens, and now the pigs, so I don't have time. And everyone knows you're supposed to paint before you bring in furniture." She tried not to stare at his legs, but the hem of the bathrobe reached only to his knees. Nice calves. Yeah, very nice.

"That's a good point. Painting should come first."

"But that's not the real reason. I can't get excited about furniture." But she was getting quite excited about watching the gentle rise and fall of his chest. Whenever he breathed in, the terry shifted to reveal more of that delicious territory. It would be so easy to walk over and slide her hands under the lapels...

"I thought women like shopping for furniture. In general, I mean."

Furniture. Right. She redirected her thoughts to the topic at hand. "It all looks the same to me—boring." Which certainly wasn't a word she'd use to describe Regan. His thighs were probably as impressive as his calves. "I'd be fine with those throw pillows you might have seen stacked in the corner, and maybe a beanbag chair. But my mom convinced me I need a couch. They'll be replacing theirs soon, and at that point my dad will bring me their old one."

"Is their couch boring?" Amusement lit his brown eyes.

Luckily her attention had been on his face at the time, so she caught that. "I'm afraid so, but then, what couch isn't? And it's not just the color, which in this case is beige. I realize you can find them in red, or purple, or paisley. I object to the basic shape—a big, bulky rectangle that takes up space and dominates the room. And is heavy. Omigod. A couch can weigh you down."

"I never thought of it that way." He sipped his wine and the bathrobe sleeve gaped open, exposing his entire forearm. His skin was tanned to a golden hue, probably a gift from his Italian ancestry.

She bet he tasted as good as he looked, but she continued the conversation as if she had no interest in licking him all over. "Couches aren't practical, either. Three people *could* sit there, but then they'd be like birds on a rail, or people waiting to have their group picture taken."

He laughed at that, and the terry lapels shifted again. *Mercy.* "No, really! In practice, only two people ever sit on a couch, even though it takes up so much floor space."

"Sometimes two people lie on a couch." Was that a challenging gleam in his eye?

"Yes, and it's crunched and crowded. A bed's better." She sucked in a breath. Where had that come from? Yikes!

"More wine?"

She glanced at the glass in her hand and discovered it was empty. Apparently she'd been chattering, ogling and drinking. The only thing she could say in her defense was that she hadn't been licking and kissing. Did she know how to draw a line in the sand or what?

Setting her glass firmly on the counter, she opened a cupboard. "I'm going to hold off on the wine for now. I'm sure the lasagna's ready. I'll dish up."

"I have an idea."

If he had one idea, she had twenty, and they all involved untying the sash of his robe. She pulled two plates out of the cupboard. "What's that?"

"Let's build a fire and sit on the floor in the living room. It's cool enough tonight for one, and I noticed you have wood."

"The Turners left me some, and I used some last month. It was a cool May." His idea sounded different and fun. And potentially dangerous.

"So what do you say? We can sit on two of those floor pillows."

"I guess that would work."

"It'll work great." He drained his glass and left it on the counter. "I'll start the fire while you serve the lasagna."

He'd already started a fire, and she had no extinguisher handy. Eating picnic style on the floor could heat things up even more. The whole setup was becoming too cozy, and she wasn't helping. She gave herself a stern reminder about the speech she was going to deliver, even if she could have done that more effectively while sitting at the dining room table.

Too late to change her mind, though. The sound of crinkling newspaper and logs settling onto the grate indicated he was into his fire-building routine. "Is the flue open?" he called out.

"No, it isn't. Pull the lever toward you."

Metal creaked. "Got it. You know, I figured you for a picnic-on-the-floor kind of woman. I couldn't ever convince Jeannette to do this, but I thought for sure you'd be all over it."

So his ex's name was Jeannette. And she didn't go for picnics on the floor in front of the fireplace. Lily should ignore that thrown gauntlet. But being a normal woman, she wanted to prove that she was more accommodating than dumb old Jeannette, the idiot who had betrayed this beautiful man on Christmas Eve. The question remained, how accommodating did Lily plan to be?

6

REGAN WASN'T OBLIVIOUS to the effect he was having on Lily. He wasn't above using it to his advantage, either. He could hardly be blamed for wearing a bathrobe that was several sizes too small for him. His only other option was a towel, and that wouldn't have helped matters.

As they settled themselves on her colorful striped pillows and balanced their plates in their laps, he was careful to keep the bathrobe closed over his crotch. This game was all about teasing, anyway, not flashing the goods. Besides, nothing could happen between them without those little raincoats. He doubted she had a supply. The woman didn't even own a make-out couch.

She was a puzzle in so many ways. Even though she couldn't stop looking at him, he could tell that she was fighting her reaction tooth and nail. She'd kissed him with enthusiasm, but she'd cautioned him that it was a mistake. He needed to find out why she'd said that, and sitting casually in front of a fire seemed like a better venue for sharing confidences than perched at the formal-looking dining table.

She'd agreed to a second glass of wine, but she was

taking tiny sips instead of knocking it back the way she had her first glass. Her speech about furniture in general and couches in particular had been entertaining. Enlightening, too. She viewed a couch as a boring anchor, so maybe she was more like his parents than he wanted to believe. Maybe, despite her dedication to these animals, she'd grow tired of being in one place and take off. He might want to keep that in mind.

For sure Lily was nothing like Jeannette. Jeannette had been perfectly okay with owning an expensive and very boring couch. Now that he thought about it, that couch might have been a symbol for whatever had been missing in their relationship. He'd asked Jeannette to marry him because he'd cared for her. Now, though, he questioned whether they'd truly been in love.

She'd appealed to him because she was deeply rooted in her hometown and she had ambition. After growing up with his rootless and unfocused parents, he craved Jeannette's lifestyle and figured they'd be blissfully happy enjoying emotional and financial stability. And a boring couch.

They'd had all that, but not much in the way of wild passion. If he were honest, he'd admit that the life they'd created as an engaged couple hadn't been very stimulating. Getting married wouldn't have changed that dynamic. She might have been bored, too, although she'd never said so. That she had sex with his best friend might have been a small indication. Ha. No kidding.

One thing he could say after spending time with Lily King—he wasn't bored. She appeared to have as many facets as the crystals hanging in her living room windows. They were the only decorations she'd put up, and there was something soothing about her minimalist approach, especially with a cheerful blaze crackling in the fireplace.

Crystals always reminded him of his mother, who loved them. As he watched the crystals reflect the light from the fire, he felt a tug of nostalgia. And he was *never* nostalgic about his parents.

His vegetarian folks also would have praised Lily's lasagna. Regan glanced over at her. "You didn't exaggerate about your cooking skills." He pointed his fork at the generous helping on his plate. "This is terrific."

"Thank you. Listen, Regan, we need to talk about that kiss."

Good thing she hadn't said that when he was drinking wine. As it was, he nearly tipped the lasagna right off his plate. But he recovered quickly enough to keep it from falling into his lap, which would have been bad on many levels. The food was hot, his privates weren't well protected and this was his only outfit.

Putting the plate safely beside him, he cleared his throat and turned to her. "Okay. Let's talk."

"You don't have to stop eating."

"I think I do. This is important."

"All right then." She put down her plate, too. "The kiss was a mistake." She looked him in the eye, her expression resolute.

"How come?"

"You broke up with your fiancée six months ago, right?"

"Right."

"I'll take a wild guess that you haven't dated anyone since then."

"Nope, and that's why I felt completely free to kiss

you. And from the way you kissed *me,* I'd say you're not dating anyone, either."

"I'm not, but that isn't the point I wanted to make. If you haven't dated since you ended your engagement, you're on target for a rebound relationship."

He blinked. Although he hadn't known what to expect from this discussion, that comment took him by surprise. "Who says?"

"It's common knowledge."

"What the hell? Is the entire population of the Jackson Hole area discussing my love life?"

"No, of course not. I didn't mean it that way. I'm just saying it's generally accepted that people suffering a breakup usually rebound to someone else for temporary comfort and a chance to get their groove back."

"Yeah, yeah, I know what you're talking about, but not everybody goes through that. And what's with me being *on target* for it? Is six months significant? Is there some timetable I don't know about?" And underneath that barrage of questions was guilt, because his thoughts this morning could easily be interpreted as a guy wanting to *get his groove back,* as she'd termed it.

"No timetable. But why haven't you dated since you broke up with Jeannette?"

"Didn't feel like it." He took a gulp of his wine. His mellow mood was disappearing fast.

"But now you do feel like it?"

"I did until this conversation started. Not sure that's still true."

"So you're not attracted to me anymore? Is that because I hit the nail on the head?"

He gazed at her, and his irritation faded. "You might have hit the nail a glancing blow."

She blew out a breath. "Thanks for admitting that."

"And for the record, I'm still attracted to you."

"Maybe because you're at the stage where you need someone and I'm handy."

"No. It's not like that." She was so much more than *handy*. Tendrils of her hair had escaped from the arrangement on top of her head, and they seemed to dance and glow whenever she moved. The freckles across the bridge of her nose beckoned to him, tempting him to kiss each and every one.

He anticipated his next move. The scent of her shampoo drifted across the space between them, drawing him closer. He longed to slide his hand up the curve of her neck, cradle her head and finally allow himself to taste her pink lips again. This time they would make that magical connection without benefit of mud or pesky pigs.

But for some reason, she was trying to give him the brush-off. He could feel it coming. But he couldn't let her think his interest was based on her being *handy*. "You're beautiful, Lily. Any man would feel lucky to be with you."

Her expression grew tender. "Not true, Regan. I don't have men beating a path to my door."

"You should."

"I understand why they don't. I'm different from most women. As you've noticed, I paint things wild colors. I mean *really* wild. I don't care about fancy clothes, or jewelry or makeup."

"You don't need those things."

"That's sweet of you to say, but I have a few other handicaps where men are concerned. I'm smart, although I've never understood why that makes men nervous. Nevertheless, it does. Earning piles of money doesn't interest me. The computer game seems to be bringing in a fair bit, but that wasn't my goal. I was just goofing around when I created it. Some guys, maybe most guys, would say I'm weird."

Her description of herself included many of the tendencies he'd worked hard to banish from his life—impulsive behavior, indifference to money, lack of defined career goals. The woman *was* on the flaky side, which should make him avoid her like the plague. Instead he wanted her so much he ached.

He decided against saying that. She was convinced that he wanted her only because they'd met when he was ready to get back in the game. "You mentioned an ex-boyfriend. What happened there?" If she could discuss his situation, then he should be able to ask about hers.

"Simple. He works for a computer-game company and he taught me how to create a game. So I did and sold it to his company. But then I lost interest."

Regan took note of that, but he wasn't ready to build a whole case on it. Making up a computer game would have been a one-shot deal for him, too. It was about electronics, not living creatures. "So then what?"

"He begged me to create more computer games and make a bunch of money. He started test-driving fancy cars and checking out coastline real estate. Then he offered to take over as my manager-slash-accountant because I obviously didn't want to deal with the financial side of my business, according to him. I didn't have a *business,* just one silly game."

"In other words, he wanted to use you to get rich."

"Pretty much. We had a big fight, and I threw him out of my funky little apartment in San Francisco."

"Which had no couch."

She pointed a finger at him. "Right. Anyway, we'd managed fine there for about a year until I sold the game and he started seeing dollar signs whenever he looked at me. Come to think of it, his affections increased in proportion to the size of my royalty checks."

"Bastard."

"He said I was wasting my talent. He even tried to make a case for a troubled world needing my happy games. That way he could pretend he was pressuring me for the good of humankind, when all he really cared about was the good of Alfred G. Dinwoody."

"That was his name? Alfred G. Dinwoody?"

"Yep. After my game became a hit, he insisted I start calling him A.G. instead of Al. He said it sounded cooler."

"And I thought I had it rough being stuck with O'Connelli."

"Are you kidding? Your name is fantastic! I've been dying to ask you where it came from."

So he told her, and naturally she loved the concept. She'd get along with his parents like peanut butter and jelly. His explanation led to more questions, and eventually she wormed the whole story of his vagabond childhood out of him.

Sometime during the telling, she suggested they eat their dinner before it got stone-cold. That made sense, so they picked up their plates and dug in while they continued to talk and drink more wine. He refreshed the fire, and she left with their empty plates while promising to bring back a package of sandwich cookies for dessert.

She didn't fancy them up by putting them on a plate,

either. She arrived in the living room with the open package and handed it to him. "Be warned that I twist them apart and lick out the filling. If that grosses you out, too bad."

He reached inside for a cookie. "I'm used to it. Half my family eats them that way." He gave her the bag.

"The O'Connor half or the Spinelli half?" She pulled out a cookie and set the bag between them.

"Some of each." He bit into his cookie. The taste rocketed him right back to his childhood. Jeannette wouldn't have dreamed of serving packaged sandwich cookies for dessert, let alone right out of the bag.

"I figure you took after your mom's side. Do any of your brothers and sisters look Irish?"

"They do. In fact, two of my sisters have red hair like my dad's, but it's not the same shade as yours."

Lily groaned. "I'm not surprised. Nobody has hair the shade of mine. It's the bane of my existence." She twisted her cookie apart.

"You're kidding, right?" This time he took out two cookies.

"Why would I be kidding? It's a shocking color that goes with almost nothing, and it's so curly it's impossible to style. Most of the time my head looks like a giant orange chrysanthemum." She proceeded to lick the frosting from her cookie.

Watching her clean the last bit of vanilla from the chocolate didn't gross him out, but it might turn him on if he paid too much attention. He'd recently been in intimate contact with that tongue of hers and wouldn't mind repeating the experience. But she seemed to think he wanted to kiss her only because he was ready to start kissing girls again and she was available.

His attraction to her didn't feel like that, but he was unsure of his position and didn't want to argue the point. That meant no kissing would happen anytime soon, no matter how her cookie-eating affected him. So he focused on the burning logs, instead, and continued the conversation. "I happen to like your hair."

"You're just saying that to be nice, but thanks, anyway."

He finished chewing and swallowed. "No, I mean it." He looked at her so she'd know he was serious. She'd already twisted another cookie apart but wasn't into the licking routine yet. "You said that the wild colors on the house and barn make you happy. When I look at your hair, especially in the sunlight, it makes me happy."

"Really?" She smiled. "That might be the best compliment a guy has ever given me. Thank you." She lifted the frosted half of the cookie to her mouth.

That was his cue to turn away.

"You *are* grossed out! I can tell!"

"Nope." He bit down hard on his latest cookie and stared into the flames while he chewed.

"Yes, you are, or you wouldn't have turned your head like that. You turned it really quick, too. I know avoidance when I see it."

He swallowed and reached into the bag without looking at her. "I'm just enjoying the fire." That wasn't working, either, because the flames were systematically licking the wood. He'd never considered fireplace logs to be phallic symbols, but they were tonight.

"Sorry, I don't believe you. If it bothers you that much, I'll eat this one the normal way. I'm putting the top back on, so you can relax."

He glanced at her. "I really don't care how you eat that cookie."

"Oh, you care, all right. It surprises me, because after the way you waded into the mud, I didn't peg you as a finicky person."

"I'm not." He hesitated, torn between admitting the real problem or letting her think he was squeamish. Finally his ego won out. "Watching you lick the frosting is…erotic."

Her eyes widened. "Oh."

"Happy, now?"

"No, I'm not happy. I apologize. I had no idea."

"We might as well get this out in the open. I'm sexually attracted to you, Lily. You seem convinced it's only a rebound situation, which means my reaction would be the same with any good-looking woman and isn't specific to you. Do I have that right?"

"Um, I guess so." Color rose in her cheeks, making her freckles stand out. "When you explain it like that, it sounds kind of insulting."

"It insults both of us."

"I suppose it does. Sorry about that."

"Apology accepted. But I assume that the possibility of me being on the rebound is why you think kissing me was a mistake."

She nodded.

"But when you kissed me, I hadn't told you about breaking up with Jeannette. Yet you said then it was a mistake and you'd explain later."

Her color heightened further and she glanced away. "I…sensed that you had some…secret anguish."

"Oh?" That sounded like bull to him. "Are you psychic?"

"A little, maybe. I pick up on things. Besides that, you kept your sunglasses on the whole time we talked this morning."

"The sun was very bright." But he had to admit he'd taken to wearing those shades more often following that last miserable Christmas, so she could have a point. He'd think about that one. "Okay, let's say that was a clue that I had a…how did you put it? Secret anguish?"

"I said that, yes." She looked uncomfortable as hell.

"What made you jump to the conclusion that it was connected to my love life?"

"Well, it was!"

"Yes, but you didn't know that until after we kissed. A *secret anguish* could apply to all kinds of things. It didn't have to be about romance gone wrong. Something's not adding up."

She swallowed. "You're right. And I can't tell you what it is."

"Why not?"

"I just can't." She grabbed the bag of cookies and pushed herself to her feet. "I need to put our clothes in the dryer."

He got up. "I'll help."

"No, don't. I'll handle it." She glanced at the fireplace. "The fire's going out."

"Want me to build it back up again?" He doubted it.

"No." She avoided looking at him. "I think it's time to call it a night, don't you?"

"Apparently so. But I can load the dishwasher while you're dealing with the clothes."

She finally met his gaze. "The dishes are taken care of. I put everything in before I brought out the cookies.

If you'll bank the fire and put the pillows back, I'd appreciate it. Good night, Regan. Sleep well."

"I doubt I will." He looked into her blue eyes. She might say she didn't want to get involved with him, but her eyes told a different story. Desire flickered there, waiting for him to fan the flames.

"Why?"

"Damn it, you know why." His control threatened to snap.

"I don't. I—"

"Because I'll be thinking about doing this." With a growl of frustration, he reached for her, cookie bag and all. He had one brief glimpse of her startled expression before he kissed her for all he was worth.

And she kissed him back. God, did she ever. Open-mouthed and frantic, she burst into flames as he'd known she would. Wiggling closer, she pressed her sweet body against his in a move guaranteed to send him into orbit.

He moaned and shoved both hands under her sweatshirt, desperate to touch her silky skin. She answered by dropping the cookies and sliding her palms under the bathrobe's lapels. Eager hands. She touched him as if she couldn't get enough. The rapid stroke of her palms against his skin drove him wild. *This. Yes, this!* His cock thrust against the terry cloth, and he wanted her with an intensity that made him dizzy.

Abruptly she twisted out of his arms. Breathing hard, she spun away from him.

"Lily..." He heard the plea in his voice. Couldn't help it.

"I don't want this."

"Yes, you do."

"Okay, I do." She gulped for air. "But it's a bad idea."

"I don't get it. That kiss was *hot*. And I've seen the way you look at me. Before dinner, while we were standing in the kitchen, I half expected you to jump my bones."

When she faced him again, her cheeks were bright pink. "I'm…I'm sorry about that. The robe is revealing."

"Something I couldn't do much about."

"I know. I apologize for ogling."

"Don't apologize! I was flattered, but I'm confused as hell. What's going on?"

She straightened her shoulders. "Let me explain. I was involved with a guy on the rebound a couple of years ago. My friends warned me not to get too attached, but I did." She took another unsteady breath. "I won't pretend that we were soul mates or anything, but I didn't expect him to take off the minute he was over his breakup."

"But…he did." He could see where this was going. He would pay for another guy's callous behavior.

"Yes, he was gone like a shot and immediately hooked up with another woman. None of that was pleasant. My friends were right. He used me to feel better about himself, and once his ego was repaired, he dropped me for someone else. Maybe I was a reminder of that bad period. Whatever. The girl who comes after a breakup usually doesn't make the cut."

"I don't know the statistics on that, but the guy was a jerk." That made two users she'd been involved with recently.

"He was, but from what I hear, the pattern is fairly

predictable, so that's why I have a rule. No rebound relationships."

"I understand why you would make that rule." He ran his fingers through his hair and dragged in some air while he tried to think this through. Something didn't add up. He gazed at her in confusion. "How do you know my ego needs repairing? All I said was that I broke up with my fiancée. As it happens, it was my decision to leave. For all you know, my ego's in fine shape."

"Then why haven't you dated before now?"

He didn't have a good answer for that, so he countered with a question of his own. "Have you dated since you broke up with your boyfriend?"

"No, but that's different."

"How?"

Her blush deepened. "Good night, Regan. I'll put your dry clothes in your bathroom. See you in the morning."

He thought about pushing the issue. She'd already proved she was a softie, as the guy had said this morning. When someone needed her, she couldn't say no. But taking advantage of her generous heart would be a lousy thing to do. It wasn't how he rolled.

They still hadn't finished their discussion, though. Why had she assumed that his ego had been bruised by his fiancée? He was missing some key fact.

Well, he had time to sort it out and examine his own motivation for wanting her. She deserved more than a rebound guy, and if that was truly his deal, then he should admit it and move on. If not, then he would convince her that this attraction was real and exceedingly specific to her, Lily King of the wild red hair and blue, blue eyes.

She'd asked him to stay through the weekend. In the next couple of days, he'd figure everything out. He wasn't about to give up on her yet.

7

IRONICALLY, LILY HAD asked Regan to stay for the weekend so she wouldn't be awake all night worrying about the animals. Instead worry about Regan and the potential of causing a problem between him and Nick kept her awake. Well, that and sexual frustration. Her resolve to stay out of the rebound trap was being seriously tested, and she was kept awake for longer than she'd like to admit.

She woke up earlier than usual, too, but that was fine because she wanted a head start on Regan. Putting on a clean pair of jeans and another of her favorite tie-dyed shirts, she pushed her feet into the boots she'd wiped off before going to bed. Then she brushed her teeth and wrestled with her hair until she had it secured with a clip at the back of her neck. The soft glow of dawn had just begun as she headed for the kitchen.

It was empty, as she'd expected it would be, which gave her time to brew the coffee, feed the horses and chickens, and maybe even chop veggies for the pigs before he woke up. The more she could accomplish, the less they'd end up doing together.

If it weren't so early, she'd call Nick Chance and confess that she'd made a mess of things. But he wouldn't appreciate being roused from sleep on a Saturday morning so that she could unburden herself. Basically she wanted his permission to tell Regan what she knew about the breakup.

As she plugged in the coffeepot, she wondered if she could find a way to take all the blame for Nick spilling the beans. She could say she pestered him until he accidentally said something that had allowed her to guess what had happened. Under the circumstances, Regan might not care if she knew, anyway. They'd moved past the acquaintance stage, so it might be fine with him that she knew.

On the other hand, Lily wasn't keen on telling Nick about the mud incident, which had led to the kiss encounter and prompted yet another kiss later on. Nick didn't need to know any of that, or that Regan had ended up wearing her bathrobe for the evening meal. She tried not to think about that too much, either. The mental image of Regan in the bathrobe still got her hot.

She probably should move past her fears about the animals rebelling and find a gracious way to let him leave today. She had no idea how to bring that up after begging him to stay, though. Besides, asking him to go implied that she was more afraid of an ill-advised relationship with him than she was worried about the animals running amok.

That didn't say much for her self-control or her priorities, now, did it? She'd have to think this over while she fed the horses. Tucking her phone in her hip pocket, she started to unlock the back door and realized it wasn't locked in the first place. Either she'd forgotten last night or Regan had beaten her to the punch, after all.

She had her answer as soon as she stepped out onto the stoop and glanced to her left, toward the corral. Regan, dressed in the dry clothes she'd left in his bathroom and wearing his hat, was working with Rex. He'd clipped a lead rope to the palomino's halter, and from the look of things, he was teaching the horse to back up on command. When Rex failed to obey, Regan waved the rope in his face until he followed the command.

Horse and man put on an interesting show, and she wasn't the only one captivated by it. Several other horses had gathered around the corral in apparent fascination. Lily couldn't resist taking out her phone and snapping a few pictures. School was in session and the pupils were in attendance, and the rising sun gave her just enough light to capture it.

She'd be crazy to send this guy away. He was exactly the person she needed to keep order in a potentially chaotic environment. Her personal issues with him faded in importance next to the benefit he'd provide to the animals in her care. So that was that. If he was willing, and she hoped to God he was, she wanted him to stay.

That decided, she watched a little longer because she didn't know how often she'd be in a position to study Regan unobserved. He and the flashy palomino made quite a pair. Regan's broad shoulders and slim hips seemed specifically suited to his jeans, boots and Western shirt. He looked great, but it was his confident movements as he worked with Rex that stirred her. Competence in any man was sexy. In someone who looked like Regan, it took her breath away.

She started to slip her phone into her hip pocket and

paused. One more picture, a close-up this time. Zooming in on Regan, she waited until she had him in profile. Damn, but he was gorgeous. Just as she clicked the picture, he turned his head and looked straight at her. Busted.

Or maybe not. From this distance he might not have been able to tell that she was taking pictures with her phone, but he certainly knew she'd been standing on the stoop watching him. She'd have to own up to that.

With a deep breath, she started toward the corral. Regan adjusted the tilt of his Stetson before leading Rex to the gate. When the horse started to crowd him, he turned and gave a quiet command. Rex stepped back.

"Awesome," Lily called out. "Looks like he's learning some manners. I hope the rest of them were paying attention."

"I think they're here because they're hoping I'll feed them. I didn't want to do that without asking, but I figured you wouldn't mind if I spent some time with Rex." He opened the gate and led the big horse through it.

"Not at all, but don't you want to leave him in there? I can feed him in the corral."

"He's had enough of a time-out. Horses really don't like to be isolated from the herd for very long. And I think Rex considers himself the leader of this one. He can't very well lead from inside the corral."

Lily fell into step beside Regan. "What if he starts acting up again?"

"We'll keep an eye on him, but let's feed the way you normally do and see how he reacts. He might be a perfect gentleman, at least for the time it takes everyone to have breakfast."

"Sounds good." She glanced over her shoulder and

discovered the rest of the horses falling in line behind Rex in Pied Piper style. "Thank you for coming out early to work with him."

"Couldn't sleep."

"Sorry."

"It's my own damn fault. You made it clear when you asked me to stay that this was a platonic arrangement."

"But then I kissed you."

"I prefer to think we kissed each other. And then I kissed you again."

Lily sighed. "And I kissed you back. My bad."

"No way was it bad." His voice caressed her nerve endings. "It was good. Very good."

Heat shot through her veins. Somehow she managed to keep walking, but her brain was filled with X-rated images.

Regan cleared his throat. "I've been doing some thinking while I was not sleeping."

"If you want to leave, I understand, although I hope you don't. I haven't made this an easy situation for you."

"You don't want me to leave?"

She looked at him. "No."

"That's a relief. All my thinking would have gone to waste if you'd decided to kick me out."

"I wouldn't do that. I wondered if you should stay or not, but then I saw you working with Rex and all the others standing around watching. Our issues aside, you're exactly who these animals need, and that's what's important."

"Thanks." He led Rex inside the barn. "Let's put him in a stall with a mare this time. He might like that better."

"Sally?"

"Maybe a younger mare. Let him dream of the days when he was a stallion."

Lily chuckled. "Okay. Gretchen, then. I'll go get her and we'll stick them both in the third stall on the left."

"I really do think he'll be fine, but let's close all the stall doors once they're situated so we can keep track of who's where."

"Gotcha." She started sorting horses, and when all were securely in a stall, she and Regan distributed flakes of hay. Rex seemed perfectly content to share a stall with Gretchen, and Lily made a mental note for the future.

She and Regan kept busy until all the horses were happily munching their breakfast. Leaving the stall doors closed meant hanging around until they were finished. She wandered up and down the wooden aisle. All seemed to be well, and a peaceful feeling settled over her. Having a buddy to help her monitor the horses was something she hadn't considered before, but it certainly lowered her stress level. She might want to take on an employee, after all.

"Have a seat," Regan said, gesturing to a straw bale at the end of the aisle, "and I'll tell you my brilliant idea."

"Okay." She sat down.

He settled next to her, but not too close. He had room to swivel a bit and look at her more directly. She did the same. Now their knees almost touched.

He nudged his hat back with his thumb. "First point—you need to set up an adoption fair. Advertise it, offer refreshments, get a bunch of people out here to look at the horses and maybe take one home."

She fought panic. "That sounds like a huge project."

"Not so huge if we get some help."

He'd said *we*, which calmed her a little. "Like who?"

"The Chance family. They put on events like that all the time to showcase their Paints. My twin sister, Tyler, is an event planner, and I guarantee she'd help. Nick would, of course, but I'll bet a few others would pitch in. What do you think?"

She listened to the horses munching, all twenty-one of them. Intimidating as an adoption fair sounded to her, if the Chance family would help, she'd do it. "That's a great idea, Regan. Thank you for suggesting it."

"Good. We can call the ranch today and see if anyone's available to discuss the details. If they are, we'll drive over and see what weekend they have free. We need to start planning and advertising now."

"But we're not ready to set a date! Rex is the only horse you've worked with, and you didn't spend much time with him. How can we set up an adoption fair when so much needs to be done with the horses?"

His gaze was steady and his voice calm. "Setting a date will give us a goal. We can concentrate on the most adoptable horses first and work with them for as long as we have."

"Okay." She pressed a hand to her chest. "But this is making me nervous. I don't know how to train a horse yet, and I'm sure I won't be as effective as you are at first. Plus I don't have a lot of extra time, as I've explained. I don't know when—"

He put a hand on her knee and gave it a gentle squeeze. "I can do most of it. We'll be fine."

"But you have a full-time job."

"True." He took a long breath. "So I'd have to train your horses during my time off, which would be evenings and weekends, or whenever I don't have an appointment scheduled. Logistically, that could be accomplished more easily if I move in here until the fair."

She gulped. On the surface, the plan was perfect. She needed help, and he was obviously good at handling horses. As a single guy with no ties, no lease and no mortgage, he was free to switch his place of lodging from the ranch to her rescue facility.

"So, Lily, what do you think?"

"I would pay you, of course."

"No, you wouldn't. You're running a charitable organization and I'm volunteering my time. If you started paying me, I'd be an employee, and I don't care for that dynamic."

"Why?"

He fixed her with a penetrating stare. "I think you know."

"The whole attraction thing."

"Right. Suppose you started paying me, and then we became involved. I'm not saying we will, but it could happen. That would be awkward."

"It would be better if we didn't get involved, but I suppose, if we're living under the same roof..." The thought made her nerves hum in anticipation.

"I won't push, Lily. I promise you that. I decided last night that wouldn't be right. You're susceptible to me, but you don't want to be."

"For good reason."

"I get that. But I've given the rebound concept a lot of thought, and while I can see why you'd think that was my motivation, it isn't. Or it isn't now." He hesitated. "It might have been yesterday, before I spent more time with you."

She blinked. "That's honest."

"I'm being as honest as I possibly can. I don't want to be like those other two guys, the ones who were only using you. I like to think I'm not like that. I like to think I see you as a person and not as a means to an end."

How she wanted to believe him.

"I know this might be difficult for you to accept after dealing with two greedy losers in a row, but I'm risking as much as you are with this arrangement."

"You are? Why?"

"I don't want you to take this the wrong way and become even more convinced that I'm on the rebound after all, but the truth is..." He paused. "I, uh, found Jeannette in bed with my...my best friend. On Christmas Eve."

"Oh...that's terrible!" She hadn't been prepared for him to confess that, and she was a beat too slow in her shocked response.

His eyes narrowed. "You already knew that."

She was afraid the truth was there in her eyes, no matter what she said. But she didn't have to confirm it by opening her mouth.

"Nick told you, didn't he?"

"It's not his fault! I wormed the information out of him! I thought you had—"

"A secret anguish. I remember."

"Please don't be upset with him, Regan. He's very protective of you and wishes you the best. I've known Nick ever since I was in junior high, and—"

"He mentioned something about that."

"We're good friends. I told him that if you and I would be working together, I didn't want to walk into a minefield without realizing it. I can be very convincing when I'm after something."

He gave her a lopsided smile. "I can imagine."

"Nick wanted us to get along, so he very reluctantly gave me the basic information. I can't emphasize enough how reluctant he was. He thinks the world of you. You're family. He didn't reveal any more than you just said. He gave me no particulars, I promise!"

"He'd have a tough time doing that when he doesn't know the particulars. Nobody does except me, Jeannette and Drake. And it'll stay that way."

"Which it should." She saw the raw pain in his eyes and longed to reach out to him, but he might think she did it out of pity.

"This explains a lot, though. You had the info on me before you asked me to spend the weekend, right?"

"Right."

"So at that point you decided I had to be on the rebound and you wanted nothing to do with that kind of deal."

"Exactly."

"But, inconveniently for you, I flip your switches."

She sighed. "You do."

"That makes two of us with that problem. But considering where we're both coming from, it could turn into a disaster. I wasn't willing to admit that before, but it's possible one or both of us could get hurt."

She allowed herself to look into his eyes again and sink into the warm chocolate depths. "True."

"I wasn't just dumped. I was betrayed, which is a whole other kind of hell. In the wee hours this morning I faced the fact that I'm at least as nervous about getting into a relationship as you are."

"Are you saying we both have something to lose?"

He nodded. "I think so, yes."

"That does shine a different light on things."

"It does." He held her gaze for a moment. "The horses are getting restless. We need to let them out."

"Sure." She stood. "So we'll keep things platonic between us?"

"I didn't say that." He got to his feet, too.

"What are you saying, then?"

"We should think it through as best we can and be honest with ourselves and each other. No secrets."

"Regan, please don't call Nick and chew him out. Put the blame for the security leak on me."

"Don't worry. I won't call him. I've only known you for twenty-four hours, and I can already see how you'd maneuver Nick into giving up information. I'm sure he thought it was the right thing to do. Obviously I was ready to tell you, anyway. No harm done."

She let out her breath. "I'm glad. I was a little worried that you'd be upset with him."

"No. From now on, though, this is between you and me. Nick doesn't need to know what's going on with us."

"You thought I'd tell him?"

"You said you were really good friends."

"Not *that* good."

Regan smiled. "Happy to hear it. Although I warn you, once our living arrangement becomes public, some people will make assumptions."

"They can assume all they want. That doesn't mean they'll be right."

"It doesn't mean they'll be wrong, either." He gave her a long look. "When I see you standing in the light pouring in through the door, your hair so bright and your eyes so soft…" His voice grew rough with emotion. "I ache for you, Lily King."

She watched in stunned silence as he turned and ambled down the row of stalls, unlatching doors as he went. No man had ever said anything remotely like that to her before, with such intensity. She might not be psychic, but she had a premonition that from this moment on, her life would never be the same.

8

FROM THE WAY the rest of the morning went, Regan concluded that he'd changed the game with that statement. The tension level between them had zipped from yellow to orange and was edging into the red zone. But he'd promised to be straight with Lily from now on. No secrets. So when he'd felt his heart shift as he'd seen her standing in a sunbeam, he'd told her the absolute truth. At that moment, he'd wanted her more than his next breath.

After that, she'd treated him with wary respect, as if he might lose control at any moment. He wouldn't, of course. But as they drove over to the Last Chance after all the chores were done, he noticed a flicker of excitement in her eyes whenever she glanced at him.

The night before when he'd been forced to wear her robe, she'd looked at him with pure lust. He'd enjoyed that, even if he'd felt a little like a Chippendales stripper. Early this morning she'd taken pictures of him with her cell phone and he'd sensed the same motivation: she was admiring the packaging, not the man inside. He wouldn't knock that because it was damned flattering, but a steady diet of it would be like eating only dessert all the time. After a while, he'd crave something more substantial.

Now, after his confession in the barn this morning, he was getting the substance he wanted. Besides the current of electricity that constantly arced between them, she was taking the time to really look at him, as if trying to see more than the obvious. He'd risked being more intense, and she seemed fascinated by that. He'd also made himself vulnerable, which was a little scary.

How strange to think that yesterday he'd been imagining them simply having a little fun together. No big deal. A few laughs. Some great sex. Parting as friends when it was over. But from what he knew of himself and what she'd told him about her background, neither of them were good at that kind of no-strings affair. They'd be kidding themselves if they tried it.

So if they became involved with each other—and on some level they already were involved—they'd both be all in. Maybe it would last two weeks, and maybe it would last much longer than that. He wasn't predicting the outcome, only the emotional investment from the beginning. They wouldn't be able to help themselves.

He pictured them standing at the top of a cliff hand in hand as they prepared to dive into a deep pool. Every time he thought about holding her in his arms again, adrenaline rushed through him. The tension here in the small confines of his truck's cab told him the moment would come sooner rather than later.

As he pulled into the circular gravel drive in front of the Last Chance's main house, he wondered if any of the people they were about to see would pick up on that tension. Judging from what he'd observed about

Sarah Chance, she would. The matriarch of the family didn't miss much when it came to those she cared about. Luckily for Regan, she cared about him. He'd always be grateful for that.

Sarah made him feel at home in this massive two-story log house, but the structure itself seemed to welcome him each time he pulled up in front. The wide center section flanked by two wings jutting out at a forty-five-degree angle reminded him of arms spread in an embrace. A covered porch lined with rocking chairs ran the length of the house and symbolized hospitality. Now that summer had arrived, evenings found the chairs occupied by any of the Chance clan who happened to drop by.

He stopped the truck and shut down the engine before turning to Lily. "How long since you've been here?"

"Oh, gosh, quite a while. I've been so busy with Peaceful Kingdom that I haven't been over since I moved back here. My parents were invited to Nick's high school graduation party, and they brought me along, but we're talking almost fifteen years ago. After that…let me think. I kept in touch with Nick off and on through email. When Jonathan Chance died in that rollover, I was at Berkeley. My parents went to the funeral, but I couldn't come home for it. I would have missed too many classes and my parents advised me not to come." She paused. "I should have, anyway."

"I'm sure everyone understood."

"Of course they did. The Chances aren't petty about things like that, but I still wish I'd made the effort. I've run into various family members in town since I've been back, and they're always nice to me."

"Have you met Pete, Sarah's new husband?"

"I have." She smiled. "They were eating lunch at the diner one day when I was there. Seems like a terrific guy, and I love the idea of the camp for disadvantaged boys that he and Sarah run every summer."

"Uh-oh. I just remembered something. That camp starts next Sunday."

"It does? Well, I guess it would. I tend to lose track of time, especially lately."

"I forgot about it until now, too, but that means we might only have next Saturday as an option for the adoption fair."

"Yikes." She blew out a breath. "That's too soon."

"Maybe not. If we concentrate on training five or six horses and get those adopted, we'll significantly reduce the overcrowding. By then you'll have the fence built. You'd be in much better shape."

"I don't know. A week…" Uncertainty shadowed her blue eyes.

"We can do it. I have several gaps in my appointment schedule next week. I won't fill them."

"No! You'll lose money!"

He shrugged. "I'll make it up later. No big deal."

"I should pay you, then."

"We've been over that. No dice. I'm not hurting for money, so let's not talk about it anymore, okay? I want to do this. It's important to me, too, now."

"Okay." She hesitated. "But do you really think we can be ready in a week?"

"Yeah, I do." Unfastening his seat belt, he leaned toward her and gave her a quick kiss. "Have faith." The kiss had been a last-minute decision, and he needed every ounce of willpower he possessed to end it immediately and open the driver's-side door.

But he'd wanted to try a small laser strike and see what happened. Apparently his strategy had the desired effect. By the time he rounded the front of the truck and opened her door, which took several seconds, she was still seated and she seemed a little dazed.

"Ready to go in?"

"Sure." She swallowed hard and started down.

He offered her a hand, which she accepted without comment. He released his hold the moment she had both feet on the gravel drive.

"That was sneaky, Regan." She glanced up at him.

"Meaning you didn't like it?"

"Oh, I liked it. But I wasn't expecting it."

That made him smile. "Aren't you the woman who told me she likes the unexpected? The one who doesn't want to be bored?"

Her expression was priceless. He'd turned her words back on her, and apparently she wasn't used to that. She couldn't seem to decide whether to challenge his statement or laugh. In the end, she laughed. "Touché."

"Just so you know, I've wanted to do that ever since you showed up at the corral this morning, but I couldn't find the right moment."

"You've wanted to kiss me all that time?"

"Not a full-out kiss, because we had stuff to do, but something quick and to the point, just to let you know I'm thinking about it."

"By *it,* are you referring to kissing…or something else?"

"Kissing."

She looked skeptical.

"That's all, I swear. If I allowed myself to think of *something else,* the drive over here would have been painful."

Her eyebrows lifted. "My, you are being honest, aren't you?"

"That's my goal. Come on." He tilted his head toward the steps leading up to the front porch. "Let's go see if the Chance contingent has next weekend available for our adoption fair. But first I need to warn you about something."

"What's that?"

"They have a couch in the living room. Don't read too much into that. They're still very interesting people."

She rolled her eyes. "This is going to turn into a thing, isn't it?"

"Yeah." He grinned at her and felt that flash of happiness he was beginning to associate with Lily. "Our first inside joke."

SARAH, HER SILVER hair styled in its usual sleek bob, met Lily and Regan at the door. She was dressed casually in jeans and a denim shirt, but Sarah could make any outfit look elegant. As she greeted them, Lily remembered why she admired this woman so much. Sarah behaved as if she'd been gifted with two of the most anticipated guests in the world, A-listers who had graced her with their presence.

When Sarah was glad to see someone, she pulled out all the stops. Rumor had it that when she wasn't glad to see someone, her reception could turn a sunny day into an ice storm. She never lost her poise, but she could freeze people in their tracks. Lily planned to stay in Sarah's good graces.

"I'm so happy about you buying Peaceful Kingdom, Lily." Sarah took her by the arm. "You were the perfect person to do it. We're all gathered in the kitchen gobbling up the last of Mary Lou's coffee cake, but she saved two big pieces for you and Regan."

"Mary Lou's still your cook?" Lily remembered her from the graduation party fifteen years ago. The feisty woman had taken Lily aside and told her not to settle for some guy who wanted to keep her barefoot and pregnant. It was good advice, and Lily had never forgotten it.

"She's still our cook," Sarah said. "I don't know what we'd do without her. She's married now, you know."

"Mary Lou? She's the one who urged me not to get married."

"And she was against it for years." Sarah chuckled as she guided Lily through the living room, which had, as Regan had mentioned, a leather couch, not to mention some heavy-looking leather armchairs. "But we have a ranch hand named Watkins who'd had his eye on her ever since he came to work for us. He's wooed her off and on, and finally, two summers ago, he convinced her to marry him."

"I'm astounded. I thought she'd never tie the knot." Lily had a brief glimpse of the large rock fireplace that anchored the living area, and she decided that a room like that needed a weighty couch and several sturdy armchairs. The high beamed ceilings, the winding wooden staircase that led to the second floor, and the immense wagon-wheel chandelier all seemed to demand substantial furniture. Lily's modest living room did not. Case closed.

"They seem pretty happy." Sarah led Regan and Lily down a long hallway lined with family pictures. "They ran off and got married on a cruise ship, so they've been threatening to renew their vows with a ceremony here at the ranch. We have a busy summer coming up, but if they really want to, I'll make it work."

Lily didn't doubt Sarah's abilities, which gave her hope that an adoption fair really could take place at Peaceful Kingdom, even within the short time frame. Usually she went with the flow and didn't worry too much about how everything turned out. But she felt more responsibility for the animals than she had for any project she'd taken on in the past. She needed more clarification. "You must be getting ready for the boys to arrive."

"We are, but we've been doing this for several years, now. We're not as panicked about having those nine kids here as we were the first couple of times. And Regan, I have to say that your little sister Cassidy is the most energetic young woman I've ever met. She'll have no trouble keeping up with those boys. I just worry that they'll disturb you, even if your room is in the other wing. They can be loud."

"I'm sure I'll be fine," Regan said.

Lily pressed her lips together to keep from smiling. She didn't think Regan wanted to move in with her specifically to avoid living on the same floor with nine adolescent boys, but that had to be a bonus. She wondered when he planned to let Sarah know he was changing his place of residence. Maybe not right now, when several family members were gathered, including his twin sister, Tyler. Lily appreciated him holding off.

When they entered a large dining room with several round tables for eight, Lily was disoriented. "I don't remember this part at all."

"It hadn't been built when Nick graduated from high

school, and I think that was the last time you were here," Sarah said.

"Wow, you have a good memory. I had to stop and go back over some dates before I could be sure about that, but I think you're right. It's been almost fifteen years."

"Jonathan and I designed this room because we had a habit of gathering all the ranch hands for lunch as a way to keep in touch on a regular basis. As we hired more hands over the years, they didn't fit in the old dining room anymore. We added this one, turned the old space into a family dining area and enlarged the kitchen and Mary Lou's living quarters."

Lily glanced around and pictured the tables filled with cowboys joking with each other while they tucked into Mary Lou's excellent meals. Although Lily would never want a big operation like this, she appreciated the ranch's contribution to the community. It employed a lot of people and was famous for taking in both animals and people who needed another shot at straightening out their lives.

Thinking about that, Lily had an epiphany. Her urge to take over Peaceful Kingdom had its roots here at the Last Chance. As a thirteen-year-old she'd been dazzled by the Chance mystique. But until now, she hadn't made the connection between the ranch's reputation for helping others and her current decision to save Peaceful Kingdom.

She decided against mentioning that now, when she was about to ask a favor. It might not come across as sincerely as she meant it. She knew now, though, that without being exposed to the Last Chance, she wouldn't have been motivated to buy Peaceful Kingdom. She wouldn't have met Regan, either.

She didn't want to put too much weight on this bud-
ding relationship, but several of her friends at Berkeley
would be raving about karma at this point. She wasn't
ready to do that, but Regan's intensity this morning in
the barn made her wonder what kind of cosmic energy
they were stirring up.

Whatever was going on, she experienced the world
more vividly as a result. The stealth kiss from Regan
lingered on her mouth and continued to send little shock
waves through her system. Her energy level was un-
usually high even though she hadn't slept much, and
she couldn't blame caffeine because she'd had only one
cup of coffee this morning. She also kept involuntarily
glancing at Regan as if needing to make that visual
connection on a regular basis. Weird. That was a new
habit she needed to break now that they would be in a
room full of people.

As it turned out, the kitchen was extremely crowded.
Sarah waved Lily to a vacant chair at the oval table before sitting down herself, but Regan remained standing,
as did all the other men.

Fortunately Lily knew most of those gathered there.
She immediately recognized dark-haired, dark-eyed
Jack Chance, and Lily had met his blonde wife, Josie,
one night when Josie happened to be checking on things
at the Spirits and Spurs, the tavern she owned in Shoshone. Josie's brother Alex stood behind the chair of
his wife, Tyler, the event planner.

Lily noticed the strong resemblance between Regan
and his twin, and she saw a look pass between them
after Lily had been introduced. Tyler's expression said
clearly *we need to talk*. Regan merely smiled.

Until this moment, Lily hadn't met Nick's wife,

Dominique, although she'd seen pictures. Dominique was even more beautiful in person. With her short hair and big eyes, she reminded Lily of a young Audrey Hepburn. No wonder Nick had fallen for her.

Morgan, Gabe Chance's obviously pregnant wife and one of Regan's redheaded sisters, greeted Lily with enthusiasm. "Yay, another redhead in the group! That makes four of us if I count Sara Bianca, which I most certainly do."

"Speaking of my favorite niece," Regan said, "where did you stash her?"

"Cassidy's watching her and the other kids so we can have a little peace and quiet while we talk about this adoption fair," Josie said. "So ignore whatever you hear from upstairs, because we all plan to."

"Everybody have coffee?" Mary Lou Simms, a little grayer than Lily remembered but just as perky, appeared with a carafe in hand. "Hey, I know you! You're the little King girl, all grown up. Nobody told me it was you. I just heard the name Lily, but I didn't put two and two together."

"You remember me?" Lily was flattered.

"'Course I do. You were smart as a whip." She laughed. "'Spose you still are. With all that brainpower, I hoped you wouldn't get married too soon and stunt your potential. You didn't, did you?"

"Nope." Lily held up her left hand. "No ring. But I see you're wearing one."

"I am." Mary Lou's cheeks turned pink. "That old coot wore me down. And I have to say, I'm not quite as opposed to matrimony as I used to be. It has a few benefits."

Jack Chance put his arm around her. "Good thing

you said that, Mary Lou, considering that every person in this room with the exception of Regan and Lily are hitched. Voicing the opposite opinion might affect your popularity."

"Nah." Sarah's husband, Pete, a lanky man in his sixties, pushed away from where he'd been leaning against the kitchen counter. "Mary Lou can voice any opinion she wants as long as she keeps making that coffee cake. Is there any left?"

"Two pieces," Mary Lou said. "And they're reserved for our guests."

"Oh, that's okay," Lily said. "Someone else can have mine."

Jack's eyebrows lifted. "Careful what you say, there, Lily King. Turning down a piece of Mary Lou's coffee cake is loaded with implications. Implications you may not have taken into consideration before you made that rash statement."

"He's right." Nick winked at her. "You're in danger of insulting the cook."

"Oh, I didn't mean to—"

"And, besides that," Nick continued, "everybody for miles around knows this is the best coffee cake in Wyoming, so if you won't at least try it, we'll all doubt your intelligence."

"Okay, then, I—"

"Furthermore—" Nick held up a third finger "—if you don't eat your cake, you'll cause a brawl in this kitchen when we all get to fighting over your share. I know you don't want any of that to happen, so you'd best eat up and be quiet."

"I'll just do that, then." She smiled at everyone and picked up her fork. The cake was incredible, so she didn't have to fake her moan of pleasure, but after that first bite she spent a solid minute praising the taste and texture, until Nick made a slicing motion across his throat and she went back to eating.

"You'll have to get used to this kind of thing," Morgan said. "I'd like to tell you that they're not always like this, but they are. You should have seen them on skis last winter. Not a one of them would agree to wear regular ski clothes. Instead they showed up for the bunny slope in jeans, sheepskin jackets and Stetsons."

"We were stylin'," Gabe said.

His wife glanced at him. "You were ridiculous."

"We were not. C'mon, guys, back me up on this one. We made a statement on the slopes, did we not?"

A chorus of agreement was followed by protests from the wives, and no telling how long the argument would have continued if Jack hadn't banged a spoon against his coffee mug. "As I recall, we gathered here to discuss Lily's adoption fair. Shall we proceed?"

"Yeah," Mary Lou said. "And you were worried about your kids making too much noise. But for the record, my Watkins was the only smart guy who wore ski pants on the bunny slope."

That started it up again. Lily thought they were hysterical. She'd known the adoption fair was necessary, but she hadn't known it would be fun. She glanced at Regan and grinned. Being connected to the Chance family was a good thing. She just hadn't realized how good.

Then she thought of something else. She'd been warmly welcomed into this group because she was with Regan. If things worked out between them, the door to the Last Chance would always be open to her. But if the

relationship went downhill, then all that lovely friend-
liness could disappear.

As Jack might explain it, becoming involved with
Regan was filled with implications, implications she
might not have considered before she rashly kissed the
guy. She'd been able to take back her rejection of the
coffee cake, but she couldn't take back those kisses.
Nor did she want to. In fact, she hoped there would be
more to come. She'd take Regan's kisses over coffee
cake any day.

9

PROUD OF HIMSELF for coming up with the adoption fair plan and suggesting the Chance family as a resource, Regan watched as the event took shape. His twin sister really knew her stuff when it came to planning shindigs like this. He loved seeing Tyler in action, her Italian heritage coming out in elaborate hand gestures as she described her vision of the fair.

Lily caught her excitement and was soon leaping in with ideas of her own. She'd create a website, a Facebook page and the graphics for a flier. Regan stood by the counter eating his coffee cake while he watched them interact, Tyler's dark head leaning toward Lily's fiery red one. Yep, this had been a great idea, if he did say so himself.

Alex made an excellent counterpart to Tyler. He volunteered to help with local publicity and organize music if they decided to have any. These days Alex handled marketing for the Last Chance, but he used to be a DJ, which meant Alex and Tyler were the couple you wanted for a successful event.

Josie offered to put up Lily's fliers around town, including at the Spirits and Spurs. Morgan had connections in the business community, too, because she was a successful real estate broker, and Dominique said she'd push the adoption fair in her photography studio and give away portraits of any horse that was adopted. Pete's experience with charity events would be valuable, too.

"I think they have it together." Jack walked over to the counter and refilled his coffee mug. "Let's talk about the horses."

"Yeah, we need to do that." Regan finished the last of his coffee cake. "We only have a week."

Jack beckoned to Nick and Gabe. "We need a confab over here. That bunch at the table will bring in the folks. That puts us in charge of the horses."

Nick topped off his coffee and turned back to Regan. "So six out of the twenty-one aren't going anywhere. That leaves fifteen that could potentially be adopted."

"Right."

Gabe nodded. "That's doable, I think. We'd have time to showcase each horse during an all-day event. You have a corral, right?"

"Yes."

"We can give each horse fifteen or twenty minutes in that corral. Three an hour works out to five hours. We can take turns so each of us gets a break and a chance to talk to anybody who's interested."

"They aren't all ready for their spotlight," Regan said. "These aren't your expertly trained Paints, Gabe. They're a little rough around the edges."

"So what kind of behaviors are we dealing with?" Jack cradled his mug in both hands. "Have you had a chance to evaluate them?"

"To some extent. Several have bad habits. They're

not well mannered on the lead, or they've tried to crowd me in the stall. A couple are biters."

Jack nodded. "I figured as much. People say they don't have the money to keep a horse, but sometimes it's more that the horse has developed bad habits and they don't know how to correct them." He looked at Regan. "You don't want to adopt out any horses that misbehave. Either they'll come back, or they'll be mistreated or passed on to some other unsuspecting person. Bad for the horse."

"I know."

"And Lily doesn't know how to retrain them yet," Nick added. "She admitted that when I talked to her on Friday. Oh, and by the way, Regan, a fence crew will be out there Monday morning to build her a paddock."

"Excellent. Thanks, Nick."

"I convinced them she doesn't have the time to wait for them to work up a detailed estimate, so they'll just give her a ballpark figure before they start. If she okays that, they'll get to it immediately."

Regan nodded. "Good. I'm sure Lily will be thrilled. The fact is, we can't have an adoption fair without a paddock. Penning the horses up in the barn for the day isn't a good idea."

"I'm still working on the issue of how we'll get them trained," Gabe said. "I could spare some time at night, but that means leaving Morgan to deal with the kids, and she gets tired now that she's PG again. Besides, I like being there for those rug rats."

"I'm in the same boat with little Archie," Jack said. "And Josie's been shorthanded at the bar recently, so she needs me to be at home when she has to go into town."

"I probably can help some," Nick said. "But I'm

coaching Lester's Little League team, so that takes up three nights next week. Luckily his Saturday game is at night, so it won't conflict with the fair."

"Even if it did, the game's more important." Regan had become fond of Lester, a small but spunky fifteen-year-old who'd been in the first batch of campers a couple of years ago. Dominique and Nick had fallen in love with Lester, and when they'd discovered he was in a dicey foster-care situation, they'd adopted him. "If you wanted to come out and train some night when he doesn't have a game, you could bring him along."

"That's an idea. And you know what? We don't have to showcase all fifteen on Saturday. This will be an ongoing process, so we should plan to do another fair later on, maybe in the early fall."

"I agree," Regan said. "If we can adopt out six or seven, that would be huge." He glanced at Jack and Gabe. "I don't want either of you to worry about anything except coming out on Saturday. Your kids are young. You have to be away from them most of the day. You don't need to be sacrificing your evenings. I can handle the training."

Jack set his empty mug on the counter. "I'm sure you can, especially if you only concentrate on six or seven horses. But it'd be a lot more convenient if Peaceful Kingdom was located on this side of town instead of in the other direction. You're going to be doing a lot of driving."

"Not necessarily." Regan hesitated. He didn't want to make Lily uncomfortable by discussing their new living arrangements while she was in the room, but she seemed to be absorbed in her conversation with the publicity team. "I don't want you guys to read anything

into this, but I've decided to stay in Lily's guest room for the time being."

"Yeah?" Nick kept his expression carefully neutral. "Does she know about this decision?"

"She does. We had a little incident yesterday where one of the geldings went after another one, and it scared her. She doesn't have the background to deal with that kind of thing, so she asked if I'd hang around this weekend. If I'm going to work with the horses in my spare time this coming week, it seems logical for me to stay on."

"Yes, it certainly does." Jack nodded and ducked his head to take a sip of his coffee.

"Absolutely." Gabe stroked his mustache, which allowed him to cover his mouth except for the corners, which were twitching. "Brilliant idea."

Jack spit his coffee back into his mug and his shoulders shook. When he looked up, his eyes brimmed with laughter. "Sorry, buddy, but your story has so many holes in it, Mary Lou could use it to strain her spaghetti. We all know why you're staying out there. The animals will benefit, but there's a lot more going on than training a few horses."

Nick grinned. "When Jack's right, he's right. Fortunately, Lily thinks you're pretty cute, too. I could tell that from the way she talked about you."

Heat rose from Regan's collar. "Is that so?"

"Yeah." Nick regarded him with amusement. "In fact, I called this one last night." He glanced over at Jack. "Didn't I, bro?"

"You did. While we were sitting on the porch drinking beer and speculating on where, oh, where Regan

O'Connelli might be, since he hadn't been seen after heading out to Peaceful Kingdom around dinnertime."

"I'm sorry I missed that conversation," Gabe said. "Morgan and I took the kids to a movie in Jackson last night so I wasn't porch-sittin' like these railbirds. But I didn't miss the way you two were shooting sparks when you walked into the kitchen."

"Yeah, Tyler noticed it, too," Nick said. "I saw that look she gave you. She's gonna want to make sure you don't hook up with another loser like Jeannette. Fortunately I can vouch for Lily. She's a good kid."

"You need your eyesight checked, Nicky," Gabe said. "She's not a kid anymore, if you get my meaning."

Regan pointed a finger at Gabe. "And you can just keep your eyes to yourself, mister."

"Classic." Jack smiled and shook his head. "Possessive and protective already. This will be fun to watch."

"Keep it down, okay?" Regan quickly glanced over at the table, but Lily and the rest of them seemed oblivious to the discussion going on over by the coffeepot. "I don't want to embarrass her."

"Neither do we," said Nick. "Don't worry. We won't make a big deal out of it. But don't you need to pack a few things before you drive back?"

"As a matter of fact, I do." He thought about the box of condoms. And clothes, of course. But the condoms topped his mental list.

"Go ahead and handle that now," Jack said. "I'll explain to Mom later that you won't be sleeping here for the foreseeable future. We'll keep it on the down-low. Get your stuff and put it out in the truck. We can say you went upstairs to see Sarah Bianca."

"Which you should, anyway," Gabe said. "SB will

be devastated if she finds out you've been here and she didn't get a hug."

"Good point. I'll make it fast."

Jack checked the situation at the table. "Take your time. They're into it, now. We'll need to break it up soon, though, or they'll be renting a jumping castle and a cotton-candy machine."

"Be back shortly. Oh, and Nick, will you be sure and tell Lily about the paddock? She'll want to thank you for setting it up."

"I'll tell her. Go take care of business, Romeo."

"Right." Regan turned to leave but glanced over at Lily one last time.

As if they'd choreographed it, Lily looked up and met his gaze. The moment was short and packed with meaning. When she turned her attention back to the notes she was taking on her phone, the corners of her mouth tipped up in a secret smile.

He had the distinct feeling that she knew he was sneaking out to pack his clothes. Unless she was psychic, though, she couldn't know what else he was going after. Then again, she'd claimed to be a bit psychic.

She confirmed that she knew he'd packed a suitcase as they pulled away from the ranch house about thirty minutes later. "That was slick, Sherlock."

"What?"

"Do you, or do you not, have a suitcase full of your stuff in the back of this truck?"

"I do."

"I figured that's what you were up to when you sidled out of the kitchen. What excuse did you give the Chance brothers so you could execute that maneuver?"

"Didn't need an excuse. Jack suggested I slide out and take care of that while nobody was looking."

"He didn't! Are you saying they know you'll be staying with me at least until Saturday?"

From the corner of his eye, Regan noticed that her cheeks were very pink. "I had to tell them, Lily. They were twisting themselves into pretzels trying to figure out how we'd get these horses in shape, but the obvious answer was for me to move in and have regular access to them so I can make the best use of my free time."

"So they think this is strictly a business arrangement?"

"Well…no. They don't think that."

Lily groaned. "I'm afraid to ask what they think it is. But I guess it couldn't be avoided. This is exactly what you warned me about."

"It's not surprising." He gave her a quick smile. "You're a caring, beautiful woman, and I'm a man with a…" He started laughing and couldn't finish.

"What?"

"A secret anguish." And he laughed some more.

She whacked him on the arm, but she was laughing, too. "I'll never live that down, will I?"

"I kind of like it. It gives me a certain Phantom of the Opera appeal."

"It used to, before you started making fun of my tenderhearted description." She folded her arms and did her best to look stern and disapproving. "See if I worry about your secret anguish anymore. Or, to be more direct, O'Connelli, *bite me.*"

He laughed so hard he almost ran them off the road. Fortunately they were still on the dirt stretch leading to the main highway into Shoshone and nobody else was coming from the other direction. "You are such a redhead. But I grew up with redheaded sisters. You can't scare me."

"You sure?"

His laughter faded. "No. You scare the hell out of me."

"I know."

"How do you know?"

Her voice grew quiet. "Because you scare the hell out of me, and I recognize the look of panic that sometimes flashes in your eyes."

"Yeah." He sighed. "I'm sure it does."

"I like you, Regan. I like you a lot."

"Ditto." He took a deep breath. "Want to know how I picture us?"

"Probably not, but now that you've asked me, of course I'll die of curiosity if you don't tell me."

"Is that a yes or a no?"

"Yes! How do you picture us?"

Now that he was about to tell her, he decided it was sort of stupid. Ridiculously romantic. Dopey, even. He shouldn't have brought it up.

"Come on, Regan. You have to tell me now."

"You'll laugh."

"No, I won't. I promise. You're not thinking of us as Romeo and Juliet, are you? Or Anthony and Cleopatra? I don't want to be a tragic couple."

"We're not. At least I hope not. But I see us as two cliff divers standing at the top of a cliff, about to dive into a deep pool. Or maybe it's a volcano, like in that old Tom Hanks movie."

"I remember that movie. He held hands with Meg

Ryan before they jumped. Are we holding hands in your mental picture?"

"Yeah." Sheesh. Good thing nobody else was around to hear this sentimental claptrap. He'd be drummed out of the manly man corps.

She was quiet after that, and he had to look over to make sure she wasn't biting her lip to keep from laughing at him and his sappy image.

She wasn't laughing. Instead she gazed at him with a soft light in her eyes. "I think that's a lovely image," she murmured.

"You do?" He waited for her to start giggling. When she didn't, he returned his attention to the road, relief easing the tightness in his chest. Guilt followed. She was a nicer person than he was. "I shouldn't have teased you about the secret anguish thing."

"I deserved it. That was way too dramatic. A cringeworthy description."

"And cliff diving isn't?"

"No, it's sweet and brave." She paused. "And I like that we're holding hands."

The warm feeling that he'd now recognized as happiness spread through him. "Me, too." Without taking his eyes from the road, he reached for her hand. She met him halfway and laced her fingers through his. They rode in silence, hands clasped, all the way back.

10

LILY THOUGHT ABOUT Regan's cliff-diving metaphor on the drive home. He hadn't said they were jumping off a cliff together into the unknown. He'd said they were diving into a deep pool. It still sounded a little scary, but they had a destination, and it involved going beneath the surface of things.

If she couldn't trust a man like Regan not to treat her as if she was disposable, then she couldn't trust anyone. She'd known from the moment she agreed to have him stay the rest of the week that she wouldn't be able to resist him for seven solid days. As they pulled up in front of the locked sanctuary gate, she realized she couldn't resist him for another seven minutes.

She'd been the one to toss up objections with all her talk about rebound relationships, so she had to be the one to remove those objections. Yes, they had a lot to do in the next few days, but the world wouldn't come to an end if they started a little bit later.

"The house and barn are still in one piece." Regan flashed her a smile as he squeezed her hand and released it. "Can't say that for the flower garden, but that was a foregone conclusion."

As she absorbed the beauty of that smile, her breath caught. She'd been drawn to him because he was gorgeous, but behind that million-dollar smile was a depth of character that she'd only begun to appreciate. She vowed to use these seven days to find out what made Regan O'Connelli so amazing.

"Lily? Are you going to let us in?"

"Uh, sure." She scrambled out of the truck and opened the gate. Standing guard, she waited until Regan had driven through before locking up again. Once the critters were all penned in, she wouldn't have to continue this little routine. But for now, because of the locked gate, no one could come to her door unannounced. Considering what she had planned for the next hour, that was a good thing.

"Are you okay?" Regan climbed out of the truck, which had been fitted with a camper shell to protect his medical supplies.

"I'm fine." And soon she'd be mighty fine. So would he, if she had anything to say about it.

"I know we didn't talk much the last few miles of the drive." He opened the tailgate and pulled out a small duffle bag. Closing the tailgate again with a clang, he turned to her. "Is something bothering you?"

"Yes, as a matter of fact, there is." She was glad he'd traded in his sunglasses for his Stetson. Looking into his eyes had become one of her favorite pastimes.

His gaze darkened with concern. "Is there anything I can do to help?"

"Yes." She kept her expression neutral, but inside she was a bottle of champagne about to pop its cork.

"What? Tell me and I'll do my best to fix whatever's wrong."

What a caring man he was. How had she ever thought he'd end up hurting her? "Let's go inside before we get into it."

"Yeah, sure." He followed her up the steps and across the small front porch with the chewed-up railing. "I'll replace that railing once the paddock is finished and Sally can't get to it anymore."

"Or I could ask the fence company to replace it. You may be too busy."

"I'll be busy, but not *that* busy. I can replace a railing. It won't take long."

"You may be busier than you think." She opened the front door and started toward her bedroom. "Come in here a minute." She used the kind of matter-of-fact tone that would suggest more home maintenance issues. But she quivered in anticipation. "I have a problem in this room."

"If it's a plumbing issue, I may need help. I'm good with the carpentry stuff and a few minor plumbing repairs, but I won't guarantee I can handle the big jobs." He set his duffle on the living room floor before continuing to follow her.

"It's not the plumbing." She turned back toward him and gestured toward his duffle. "You might want to bring that with you."

"It's only my clothes. I don't have any tools in there or…anything…" He stood in the middle of the living room and stared at her as comprehension dawned. "Lily?"

"Does your duffle have anything in it besides clothes?"

His breathing changed. "A few other things. Shaving gear, a toothbrush." He shrugged, but his gaze never left hers. "The usual. Was there something in particular you wanted to know about?"

"There is." She swallowed. "You might not have brought it. If you didn't, then I guess my…problem will have to wait." Her heart beat so fast she grew dizzy.

Heat flared in his dark eyes. "I think I might have what I need to fix your problem."

"Good." She struggled to breathe. "Then would you please come in and evaluate the situation?" She turned and walked on shaky legs through the doorway into her bedroom. Sunlight streamed in through the set of double-hung windows on the west wall. This wouldn't be a scene enacted in the dark, with shadows to hide in. But with Regan, she didn't need shadows. Taking the clasp from her hair, she tossed it on the bedside table. Then she turned and watched him walk into the room.

He paused just inside the door and the duffle slipped from his fingers, hitting the floor with a soft thud. "The sun…" He cleared his throat. "The sun is all around you. Just like this morning…in the barn."

"I'll never forget the way you looked at me, Regan. And what you said."

His voice dropped to a low, urgent murmur. "I still ache for you, Lily."

"I'm counting on that." She untied the tails of her shirt and slowly began unbuttoning it with trembling fingers. "Because I ache for you, too." Sliding her shirt off, she let it fall noiselessly to the floor. "Are you ready to take that dive?"

"God, yes." He closed the distance in two long strides and cupped her face in both hands. For a long moment he gazed into her eyes as his thumbs lightly caressed her cheeks. The air seemed to crackle between them. "Thank you for trusting me enough to be here."

She flattened her palms against the solid wall of his chest and absorbed the warmth. "Your heart's beating fast."

His mouth tilted in a soft smile. "And I'm not even kissing you yet."

"I noticed that. Are you planning to get around to it?"

"Oh, yeah. But I have a feeling that once I start kissing you, all hell is going to break loose. It sure did last time." He combed his fingers gently through her hair. "You're potent."

"Backatcha."

He sucked in a breath and his attention dropped to her mouth. "Oh, Lily. This is going to be wild."

"Good."

His fingers tightened on her scalp as his gaze met hers. The fire in his eyes burned with enough heat to melt the clothes off her body. "See how you are?" His voice roughened. "No wonder I'm half-crazy with wanting you, Lily King. But that's why I thought that maybe, before we got into it, I should apologize in advance if I…forget myself and become a little…out of control."

A tsunami of lust slammed into her. "Now, Regan. Kiss me *now*."

With a groan, he captured her mouth with such urgency that she clutched his shirt in both hands. Her world began to tilt. Oh, yes. Oh, *yes*. His tongue, deep and questing, his lips demanding all she had to give, his fingers pressed against her jaw, coaxing her to open to him—she surrendered to it all with reckless abandon.

His mouth found the pulse at her throat and nipped

the soft skin there, sending a jolt of desire straight to her core. She grew moist and pliable, eager to offer herself to him in every way a woman could offer herself to a man.

And he took, continuing down the slope of her breast. Somehow her bra had been eliminated, but she couldn't remember how or when. Bending her backward over his arm, he teased her aroused nipple with his lips and tongue. She arched shamelessly into his caress and held his head there, right *there*. His cheeks hollowed as he rhythmically sucked, and each firm tug heightened the pressure coiling within her.

When she thought she would surely come apart in his arms, he eased his mouth from her breast and began a new journey. Holding her steady with hands bracketing her hips, he crouched down as he trailed kisses from the underside of her breast to the fastening of her jeans.

"Undo this." His hot breath wafted against her skin as his tongue dipped into her navel and he kneaded her backside with supple fingers.

She barely managed the job. Her hands shook as she fumbled with the metal button.

"Hurry." He nibbled and licked her fingers as she worked.

His questing mouth gave her a vivid preview of what he intended once her jeans were undone, and her hands trembled even more. "You're…you're not helping."

"I'm an impatient man." He thrust his tongue into the crevice between each of her fingers.

Her womb clenched in response. Finally she worked the button free and reached for the zipper.

"Never mind." He nudged her out of the way with his chin and caught the tab between his teeth.

Continuing his sensuous massage through the soft denim of her jeans, he drew the zipper down. The ragged sound of their breathing mingled with the rasp of interlocking metal giving way. Anticipation pounded through her veins and threatened to shove her over the edge before he even touched her.

The zipper reached the end of its track. Deft hands slipped inside the waistband of both jeans and panties and eased them over her hips and down to her knees.

She quivered, and a soft moan slipped unbidden from her lips.

His voice was tight with restraint. "You might want to hold on, pretty lady." As he gripped her from behind, his fingers gently coaxed her forward. Then he leaned in and touched her throbbing pulse point with the tip of his tongue. "So beautiful." He made a slow circle, and another.

She cried out and clutched his head in both hands as a spasm shook her and her knees nearly buckled.

Tightening his grip, he began a steady, relentless assault. The liquid sound of his talented mouth caressing her, whether the pace was slow and languid or rapid and urgent, never stopped. She began to pant as heat sluiced through her veins and gathered, heavy with promise, at the quivering juncture of her thighs.

Then he shifted his angle and delved deeper, tasting her so intimately that she gasped. His boldness should have shocked her, but she was too far gone, too immersed in the whirlpool of pleasure he'd created. She wanted what he was giving her—all of it.

As her climax bore down on her, she dug her fingertips into his scalp and arched her hips, shamelessly inviting him to take everything he wanted. He ramped up the pressure one more notch, and she came, and came hard, in a spiraling surge that lifted her to her toes and wrenched a long, keening cry from her throat.

And still he didn't stop. Burrowing deep, he brought her upward again, until her breathless cries filled the room and she lost track of whether she was standing or falling. Then strong arms swept her up and laid her, quivering and moaning, on the bed.

He kissed her mouth, her closed eyelids, her cheeks and her hair as he crooned soft words of praise. Yet he was the one who deserved praise. She would give it, too, if she ever recovered, if her vocal cords ever began functioning again and her lungs could drag in enough air.

For now, all she wanted was to lie here with her eyes closed and savor the wonder of an orgasm to end all orgasms. And she thought she'd understood what sexual pleasure was all about. Not even.

At some point he stopped kissing her and the next thing she felt was her boots coming off. She thought that was funny, because she'd forgotten she was still wearing them. But she didn't have the energy to laugh. Once the boots had hit the floor, he pulled off her jeans and panties.

Then she heard nothing but silence. Wondering if he'd left the room, she opened her eyes to discover him gazing at her. She didn't mind. After what they'd just shared she could hardly play the modesty card.

Besides, judging from his expression, he was mighty happy with what he saw. He looked—there was no other word for it, although thinking it made her blush— awestruck. She'd never experienced that before. It felt kind of nice, but strange, really strange.

He swallowed. "You're so beautiful, Lily."

Now she really was blushing. Letting him stare at her as if she had an amazing body was one thing, but hearing him say it out loud was going a little far. "Thanks, but you don't have to say that just because we—"

"It has nothing to do with that. Yeah, I wanted to get you naked for my own selfish reasons, but I hadn't counted on how seeing you that way would affect me. I was too busy a while ago to pay attention, but believe me, I'll pay attention from now on. You're magnificent."

"Magnificent? No." She rolled to her side and propped her head on her hand. "I'm reasonably good-looking." She swept a hand down her body. "Except for all the freckles."

"Are you kidding me? Your freckles are the best part of you." He grinned. "Well, okay, maybe not the *best* part."

"You're referring to my brain, of course."

He continued to smile as he unbuttoned his shirt. "Of course."

"I always wanted to be that tanned girl you see in bathing-suit commercials, but I don't tan. Mostly I look as if someone sprinkled me with nutmeg."

"Or cinnamon." He unsnapped the cuffs of his shirt, took it off and tossed it on the old rocker she had sitting in a corner of the room. "I like nutmeg and cinnamon."

Talk about spicy. The guy could fill out a white cotton T-shirt. A few minutes ago she'd thought her sexual urges were tamed for now, but watching him undress taught her that wasn't exactly true.

"Nutmeg and cinnamon remind me of pumpkin pie. You know, your hair is sort of pumpkin colored, so it all fits." He reached behind his back and grabbed the neck of his T-shirt to pull it over his head.

"FYI, most girls don't like to think their hair is the color of a pumpkin, even if it is."

"Uh-oh. Did I lose points?" His voice was muffled as his head disappeared temporarily inside the T-shirt.

By the time he'd pulled it off and tossed it on the rocker with the other one, she'd dismissed the pumpkin-colored-hair remark. Regan O'Connelli stood before her, a tousle-haired, shirtless cowboy fantasy if she'd ever seen one. She gazed upon the bounty he presented so casually, as if the sight of him half-naked wouldn't set her heart to thumping.

"No, you didn't lose points." She couldn't stop staring. Women bought calendars with photos of guys like this, men with broad shoulders, powerful pecs, washboard abs and a sprinkling of dark hair as a final touch. But Regan was no two-dimensional pinup. He was the real deal—irreverent enough to make her laugh, sexy enough to send her libido into overdrive and sentimental enough to hold images of emotional cliff diving close to his heart.

"I'm glad." He sat on the rocker and pulled off a boot. "I'd hate to lose points at a critical time like this." His muscles bunched as he took off the second boot.

"I wouldn't worry about it." She considered going over to help him with the rest of the process, because she desperately wanted to touch him. At last she'd be allowed, probably even encouraged, to smooth her hands over the sculpted planes of his body.

But if she stayed where she was, she could watch him take off the rest of his clothes, which would give her a visual that she'd cherish forever. It wasn't every day that a girl had such a fine specimen of manhood undressing in her bedroom.

After pulling off his socks, he stood and walked barefoot over to the duffle he'd left by the door. Unzipping it, he reached inside, took out a box and held it up. "Could this be the item you were asking about earlier?"

"Uh-huh." Seeing the box in his hand and knowing he'd soon be using its contents brought her right back to the trembling anticipation she'd felt when he'd first walked into her bedroom.

"Didn't know if I'd need these." Opening the box, he held her gaze as he walked over to the bed.

"Really? You couldn't tell I was folding like a cheap card table?"

His smile flickered. "I thought maybe you were, but sometimes when you desperately want something, you imagine what isn't there."

"It was there." A tremor of desire ran through her, making her hot and shaky. She lay back on the bed and drew in a deep breath. "Still is."

His hungry gaze swept over her, lingering on her tight nipples and flushed skin. "I can see that." He took out a packet and laid it on the bedside table. "You can open that if you feel like it."

"Not quite yet, cowboy. Not until I've had my hands…and my mouth…all over you."

That got the reaction she was hoping for. He peeled off his jeans and briefs in no time.

Her eyes widened as she beheld the gift she was about to receive. Regan O'Connelli had been blessed. And so had she, because for a solid week, that spectacular equipment would be hers to command. She couldn't get much luckier than that.

11

REGAN WAS A huge fan of making love in broad daylight, but he'd never found a woman who agreed with him. Until now. Lily hadn't suggested pulling the curtains or lowering the blinds. Instead her blue eyes sparkled as she demanded that he stretch out on her blue flowered quilt, smack in the middle of a patch of sunlight.

He didn't much care if he was illuminated, but when she straddled his thighs and sat there surveying the territory, those same sunbeams played with her curly red hair. He would still want her if she cut it all off, but he hoped she wouldn't do that, because that hair symbolized her in a way he might never be able to explain. Maybe it was the shockingly bright color, or the riotous curls, or her decision to keep it long so it fanned out around her shoulders in such dramatic fashion.

The sunlight also lovingly showcased her breasts. They weren't large, but they were sweetly curved, tipped with rosy nipples and dusted with nutmeg and cinnamon freckles. Eventually he'd kiss every single freckle on her pale skin. But now she proclaimed it was her turn to kiss him, and he wasn't about to deny her that.

When she leaned forward, her stomach bumped his erect cock. She settled lower, brushing against it as if she had no idea what she was doing. Slowly she stretched down far enough to nibble on his mouth as her body swayed over his. Her tight nipples tickled his pecs, along with locks of hair that tumbled over her shoulders and onto his chest. And always, always, her flat stomach slid against his throbbing erection.

Each time her flushed skin came in contact with the head of his penis, the sensation was that of warm silk caressing that increasingly sensitive spot. He stroked her smooth back and squeezed her firm backside. Seeking to even the odds, he allowed his fingers to stray, seeking that moist cleft he'd so recently tasted.

"No." She nipped gently at his bottom lip. "Not allowed."

"I think you like it." The deeper he probed, the wetter she became.

Her breathing hitched. "Stop. I want to concentrate on you."

He loved knowing he could affect her that way. He kept stroking. "Don't mind me. Just keep doing whatever you're doing, and I'll keep doing whatever I... Ouch! That's my earlobe!"

"And those are my teeth."

"Sharp little dudes."

"I'll make it better." She sucked on the spot she'd bitten.

"Mmm." He hadn't known his earlobe was an erogenous zone. Maybe with Lily every inch of his body was an erogenous zone.

Her breath warmed his ear. "Move your hands away

from my happy place, cowboy. It's my turn. I promise you'll be glad you gave me one."

That sounded promising, so he slipped his hands free and stroked his damp fingers up and down the backs of her thighs. "Can I do this? I love touching you, Lily. Your skin feels…almost as if it's humming."

"I know." She licked a path down the side of his neck. "And it's your fault, too. It's like I stuck my finger in a light socket. But I'm going to make you come, and then you'll be in the same shape as me."

He groaned as she continued to tease him. He didn't want to come yet. She could play around if she wanted to, but he wanted the joy of sinking into her and creating that ultimate connection. That was important to him.

But he was in danger of forgetting what was important as the underside of his cock grew slick with the moisture that gathered on the tip in response to her casual, seemingly accidental, touch. It was no accident, he was sure, and his balls drew up, aching with anticipation. At last she began nibbling lower, trailing kisses along his collarbone and gently biting his nipples.

He hadn't known that would make his bad boy twitch, but it did. Maybe whatever she did with her mouth would have that effect, but he was yearning for one certain caress. He hoped that was part of her plan, but if she didn't go that route, he might spontaneously erupt just thinking about her hot mouth taking him throat-deep.

No, no spontaneous eruptions. He clenched his jaw and stopped stroking her satiny back because he felt the need to grab a handful of her comforter in each fist. She made agonizingly slow progress down past his ribcage to his abs. His cock waited, rigid but under control, until she followed his example and dipped her tongue into his navel. *Damn*. His penis jerked. His body trembled, and by some miracle he didn't come.

He almost told her to stop right there and get the condom, but he wanted… Oh, he really hoped that she'd… Ah… Her mouth closed over his much-teased cock and slid down, down, down, until the vibrating tip touched the back of her throat. His heart beat like a wild thing, and breathing became his second most difficult task—not coming being the first. But this was what he'd been waiting for, what he didn't want to miss if he could hold out. If he could stand the pressure when she… began to suck.

His eyes rolled back in his head. He wasn't sure if it was her technique—wonderful!—or his supersensitized cock, but this felt like the best he'd ever had. He was tempted to let her finish it. So tempted. His body clamored for release. But then he wouldn't know how it felt to be joined with her in that most basic way. He couldn't explain why it was so important to him. It just was.

Putting a stop to the joy she was bringing him was easier said than done. He made several attempts, but then she'd use her tongue a certain way, or scrape her bottom teeth gently along the lateral ridge, and he'd be lost again.

Finally he gripped her head with firm purpose and lifted her away. "No more." His voice sounded like a rusty hinge.

"Is something wrong?"

"No." He gulped in air. "It's so right it's scary. But I want… Please get a condom. Please."

Her voice was gentle. "Sure."

As if she understood. He'd believe it. They had so

much to learn about each other, but in this it was as if they'd always been linked. Crazy thinking. But he couldn't say it wasn't true.

She put on the condom, which was a good thing because he might have fumbled the job. He was still lying there panting and holding on to her quilt for dear life. But when she'd finished, calmness settled over him.

She would have straddled him, but he stopped her. "Lie back, sweet Lily. It's my turn again."

Maybe she saw the sense of purpose in his eyes, because she stretched out beside him. When he rose over her, she welcomed him into the haven of her arms and the shelter of her body with a knowing smile.

He found his way with unerring precision. Gazing into the twilight blue of eyes glazed with passion, he drove home. He watched the spark ignite in her and fed that flame with steady, sure strokes. He didn't speak. Neither did she. Their bodies said all that needed to be said.

Her breathing quickened and her lips parted. "Yes," she murmured.

"Yes," he echoed as he felt her body rise under him. He pumped faster and she tightened around his cock. "Yes, Lily."

"Yes!" She arched in his arms, and he loosened the iron grip that had kept him in control. One more thrust, two, and he surged into her with a bellow of satisfaction that mingled with her cries of release. Burying his cock deep in her body, he shuddered in the aftermath of a climax that felt absolutely, completely right.

So much in his life had gone wrong, but in this golden moment, with the sun warming his shoulders, he was happy. Perhaps a man couldn't ask more than that.

LILY BLAMED LACK of sleep the night before, but somehow she and Regan ended up wrapped in each other's arms and oblivious to the rest of the world for the rest of the afternoon. The sun was low in the sky when she woke up to a crunching noise just outside the bedroom window.

Regan obviously didn't hear anything. He held her close, his breathing shallow, his eyes closed. Slowly she extricated herself from his embrace and eased out of the bed without waking him. Poor guy was dead to the world.

It didn't take her long to figure out where the strange sound was coming from. Sally peered through the window for a moment before resuming her snack, which was the bedroom windowsill. That was new. Until now, the horse had eaten only the porch railing.

Lily glanced back at her queen-size bed, where Regan slept on. He probably needed the rest. For all she knew, he hadn't had a decent night's sleep for six months. Stress could do that to a person. But after the stress-relieving afternoon they'd shared, he might sleep for twelve hours.

Locating her go-to sweatpants and a sweatshirt, she decided to put on her socks and boots, because she'd learned the hard way that it wasn't smart to deal with a horse either barefoot or in flip-flops. The first time she'd been stepped on while wearing flip-flops, she'd been lucky and hadn't broken any toes. She wasn't willing to trust her luck that way again.

But what to do about Sally? Lily admitted that Sally destroying the house and Buck obliterating the garden had gotten old. The paddock was an excellent idea, and she was embarrassed that she hadn't thought of it before.

The horses would still have a measure of freedom, but they wouldn't have access to the entire property. Horses shouldn't be allowed to chew on the house. They could munch on wild grass instead of whatever had struggled to grow in the flower bed.

Lily let herself out of the house as quietly as possible before crossing the porch and walking down the steps. She had to avoid two piles of horse manure on her way around to the bedroom window where Sally was helping herself to the windowsill. Normally Lily would've been on poop patrol with the little tractor parked behind the barn, but today she'd been otherwise occupied. Mmm, had she ever.

It occurred to her that normal people didn't live this way, with animals free to destroy property and leave their little offerings where someone might step in them. She might have come to that conclusion eventually, but maybe not before some disaster that was bigger than a chewed-up building. Thank heaven for Regan O'Connelli, although if Nick had come out here on Friday he probably would have advised her to change her ways.

But Nick didn't have time to help out regularly at Peaceful Kingdom. Besides his work at the clinic, he had a wife and a fifteen-year-old who desperately needed him to provide fatherly guidance. Nick would have advised her to hire some employees, which she might do, anyway, but Regan had been available to move in and prop up this teetering operation immediately.

When she thought about how she'd resisted her attraction to him because she'd worried about a rebound relationship, she had to shake her head. If she did turn out to be a rebound for Regan, so what? He wasn't the kind to use her and dump her, and he was offering to help her turn this dicey situation into a workable rescue operation. If she could help him through this difficult time in his life, then she would, without selfishly worrying about whether she'd get hurt in the process.

Rounding the corner of the house, she approached Sally, who glanced at her with disinterest before resuming her meal. The mare had probably chosen this end of the house because the pig wallow was on the other end. In general, the horses had avoided the pigs, and vice versa.

The pig wallow should be moved, too, now that Lily thought about it. She'd dug it there so Wilbur would be close to the shelter of the house and she could keep an eye on him. But a sturdy pen a distance away with added protection from the elements made more sense. And the pigs, much as she hated to say it, would have to be in separate pens at mealtime. She'd caved and given Harley more food this morning, which was the only reason he hadn't gone after Wilbur's dish.

With a sigh, she walked over and caught hold of Sally's halter. "I'm dealing with a steep learning curve, Sally, old girl. Good thing a knight in shining armor showed up. Come on, now, come away from the windowsill." She gave the halter a gentle tug.

The mare stopped chewing on the wood.

"Excellent. Now let's go back to the barn, okay?" She tugged again.

Sally planted her feet and gave Lily a look that plainly said *Make me.*

"Oh, for heaven's sake. Let's go." Lily pulled with more force.

Sally jerked her head up so quickly that she dislodged Lily's grip. When Lily made a grab for the halter, Sally tossed her head and backed up with a snort.

"Okay, you're away from the windowsill. That's a start." She thought of trying to move the horse with the flapping technique, but of course her sweatshirt didn't have tails. Besides, backing Sally all the way to the barn didn't seem like the way to go.

As Lily stood with her hands on her hips and tried to figure out a feasible plan, the mare walked back over to the windowsill and took another bite.

"Damn it, Sally!" Lily made another grab for her halter, and Sally moved deftly out of the way. Then she stood there, tail swishing and brown eyes placid. She seemed to be waiting patiently for Lily's next move in the chess game they were playing.

"Got a problem?"

She turned as Regan, shirtless and sexy, approached. In her frustration with Sally, she'd forgotten that she might be disturbing him. "I didn't mean to wake you."

"No big deal. Need some help with that animal?" He'd pulled on his jeans and boots and come to her rescue, but clearly a shirt would have taken more time than he'd wanted to spend.

Considering the potent image he presented in that outfit and how it immediately affected her with a case of raging lust, she forgave him his cocky grin. "She's determined to chew on the windowsill. I guess it tastes better than the porch railing. She's being stubborn about going back to the barn."

He paused about ten feet away and folded his arms across that beautiful bare chest. "I can see that."

"Do you think you could catch her and take her back to her stall? I'm not having much luck, and I don't want her to destroy any more of this windowsill."

"I could, but it would be better if you did it."

"So far she's defied me. If she had hands instead of hooves, I think she would have flipped me off."

He nodded. "She does have that look in her eye. How about this? Instead of going over and trying to grab her halter like you've been doing, you—"

"You were watching the whole thing from the window, weren't you?"

"Yeah. I heard her chewing and wondered what you'd do about it. When I realized she wasn't going to mind you, I decided to come out. We don't want to let her think she's the boss of you."

"Even if she is."

"She won't be for long. How about if you walk over there slowly, arms at your sides, and talk to her in a nice, calm voice as you approach? She might stay right there."

"It's worth a shot." Although at first she'd been relieved that he might handle the problem, she recognized this was better. She needed to learn how to control the horses, and he was conveniently here to teach her.

Turning back to Sally, she opened the conversation and began walking. "Hey, girl, you really don't want to chew on that windowsill, even if I did use environmentally safe paint on it. You have green flecks in your teeth, and I have to say, that's not a good look, especially at your age."

Behind her, she heard Regan's soft chuckle. "That's good. Make sure you're completely nonthreatening in your body language."

She did a body check and relaxed her shoulders. "Sally, babe, let me also appeal to your generous nature. If you keep chewing up my house, I'll be out some money for repairs. If you stop the chewing, I'll have extra money to spend on some nice perks around here. What would make you smile? Ribbons in your mane? A little bling on your halter?"

"She's listening," Regan said. "See how her ears are pitched forward?"

"Yep. I'm almost there. Now what?"

"Walk past her head, turn slowly toward her and casually stroke her neck. And keep talking. As you talk, work your way up her neck, scratch around her ears and stroke her muzzle, but act like you have no desire to grab the halter. And keep—"

"I know. Keep talking."

"Right. Your goal is to eventually take hold of the halter without making any sudden movements. Once you have it, cluck your tongue and start walking. Make sure your mind-set is that she'll follow. Assume she'll come with you, and don't jerk or tug."

"This feels like Jedi Knight training." She walked past Sally's head and slowly turned toward the horse.

"It's not so different from that. There's a lot of mental stuff going on when you work with horses. They pick up on your moods and your body language so well that you'd swear they can read your mind. If you're feeling uncertain, they won't want to do a single thing you ask. So think success."

"Okay." She continued to talk to Sally while visualizing that this interaction would go smoothly. She began stroking the mare's neck and eventually worked her way to Sally's muzzle. She could do this. Sally would obey her. When Lily thought she'd loved on the horse enough, she took hold of the halter, clucked her tongue and started walking toward the barn.

Sally followed.

Lily wanted to shout and punch her fist in the air, but that would be counterproductive. She settled for smiling at Regan in triumph.

He answered with a wide grin and gave her a thumbs-up. Then he ambled over and joined her as they headed to the barn. "Well done."

"You're a good teacher."

"I learned from the best. Ever hear of a horse trainer named Buck Brannaman?"

"Nope."

"He's the original horse whisperer, and I attended a clinic he gave back in Virginia. I haven't mastered all his techniques by any means, but he helped me tune in to the horse psyche, and that makes me a better vet. And in some ways, maybe a better man."

She eyed him. "For the record, I'm sure you were already a darned good man."

"Thanks, but there's always room for improvement."

She took a deep breath. "In my case, too. I realized when I walked out to confront Sally, that I don't give a damn if this turns into a rebound relationship. That was a selfish concern and I'm over it. The animals are lucky to have you here, and so am I. You're welcome for as long as you want to stay."

He walked quietly beside her, not saying anything. When he finally spoke, his voice was rough with emotion. "Thank you, Lily. That…that means more to me than you can ever know."

Maybe so, but she had an idea why her words had that effect. Perhaps he didn't realize it himself, but like the animals in her care, he desperately needed someone to want him again.

12

AFTER POLISHING OFF the roasted portobello-mushroom sandwich Lily fixed him for lunch, Regan decided eating vegetarian meals for a week wouldn't be bad at all. Turning into a carnivore after he'd left home twelve years ago might have been more of an act of rebellion than a dietary preference. It hadn't hurt that he'd been starving to death, though. Between the trip out to the Last Chance and all the fun they'd had in bed, they'd blown right past the normal lunch hour.

But now that one hunger was satisfied, the other one was making itself known. He and Lily had eaten their mushroom sandwiches at the formal dining table because she didn't have anywhere else to eat—other than the throw cushions from the night before. She'd taken the end seat and he'd grabbed the one on her right.

He'd also wolfed down his meal like a man who hadn't eaten in a week. Sex usually had that effect on him, which was why he often raided the refrigerator afterward. This time he'd been too worn out, but in a really good way, to do that.

They'd spent the meal discussing a training schedule,

which was supposed to begin in fifteen or twenty minutes. If they kept to that schedule, they should be able to
work with two different horses this afternoon before it
was time to feed the animals. As Regan observed Lily
finishing her sandwich, he had some very unworthy
thoughts that involved deviating from the plan.

She swallowed her last bite and caught him watching her. "What? Did you want the last bit of mine? Are
you still hungry?"

He laughed. "At the risk of sounding like a cliché,
the answer is yes, I'm still hungry, but not for food."

"Oh." Her gaze locked with his. "I see."

"But we have a hell of a lot to accomplish, so…"

"True." She gave him a once-over. "But now I'm
thinking about having sex with you instead."

"You weren't before?"

"Sure I was. But knowing you've been thinking
about it, too, is a whole other thing, if you know what
I mean."

His cock twitched. "I most certainly do." She was
still wearing those easy-access sweatpants.

"It would help if you'd go put on your shirt while I
clear the table. Sitting here with you half-naked is bound
to get a girl all juiced up."

"Nice to know I'm appreciated." His cock began to
swell.

"Oh, you definitely are, but we need to get going."
She stood. "So put on your shirt before I forget myself
and grab you."

"Okay." But he smiled as he walked into the master
bedroom. She couldn't go around delivering lines like
that and expect him to be a good boy and do as he was

told. Comments like hers inspired him to be a very bad boy, indeed.

But he could be bad and still hold to the schedule. She might not believe that, so he'd have to prove it to her. The benefits to that were many, including setting the stage for more such encounters. They'd both be able to concentrate on work much better if they took occasional breaks to release some tension.

He returned wearing a shirt just as she'd finished wiping down the table with a damp dishrag. He pointed to a place in the middle of the table. "Missed a spot."

"Are you sure? We sat at the end. We didn't even use that part of the table."

"Yeah, right there." He moved a chair aside to give her access.

She came over and peered at the area he'd indicated. "Maybe there is something left over from another meal. Oh, and FYI, buttoning your shirt would be a good thing, too. You still look like a *Playgirl* centerfold."

"Think so, huh?"

"I'll bet you're doing it on purpose to get me hot." Leaning over the table, she scrubbed at the nearly invisible spot he'd pointed out.

He coughed to cover a moan. "Is it working?" He unbuttoned his jeans.

"I'll never tell."

"Let's see." Stepping closer, he caught her around the waist.

"Hey!"

He slid his free hand neatly under the waistband of both her sweats and panties.

Her breath caught. "I thought we agreed to…Regan…"

"What, Lily?" Pulling her against the erection straining the zipper of his jeans, he thrust his fingers deep. She was slick and hot. Ready.

"Work."

"We will." He breathed in the scent of her hair and the musk of her arousal. "This won't take long."

"That's what you think." She gulped for air as he continued to probe her heat. "Once you get me back in that bedroom, we'll be in there for—"

"We're not going back to the bedroom."

"Then where are we going?"

"Right here. If we stay out of the bedroom, we'll be fine." He stroked faster. "Come for me, pretty lady."

"You're…crazy." She braced her hands on the table and widened her stance. "But that feels so…good."

"Thought you'd like it." Closing his eyes against the intense pressure in his groin, he pumped rapidly until she began to whimper and tighten around his fingers. "Let go," he murmured.

"I… Yes, there. *There!*" Gasping, she came, massaging his fingers with each contraction.

Gritting his teeth against the demands of his own body, he stayed with her until her tremors subsided. Then he slowly withdrew.

Hands still braced on the table, her face hidden by her curtain of red hair, she took a shaky breath. "Great for me. Not so great for you."

"It will be. Stay right there." Quickly unzipping and shoving his jeans and briefs down, he rolled on one of the two condoms he'd stuffed in his pocket when he went after the shirt. From now on, he planned to have one with him at all times.

Then he drew her sweats and panties down, exposing her creamy backside, which was also dusted with cinnamon and nutmeg. He longed to kiss her there, but this episode wasn't about leisurely kisses. There would be other times. Many other times.

She sucked in a breath. "Regan?"

"Lean over," he murmured. "Arch your back and raise your hips." He nearly came when she did as he asked, resting her upper body on the table and presenting him with an exotic view of his destination—pink, glistening and blatantly inviting him inside.

He certainly planned to accept that invitation, but the angle was different and he didn't want to hurt her. Breathing hard from the effort to maintain control, he grasped her hips, eased partway in and paused.

She moaned softly.

"Did I hurt you?"

"*No.* I want more."

He gave her that and fought to hold back his climax. Sweat beaded on his chest.

"More. I want it all, mister."

He sank in up to the hilt and groaned at the pure pleasure of it. He swallowed. "Still okay?"

"This is *amazing.*"

She sounded surprised. Hadn't she ever tried it this way before? "But surely you've—"

"He…he wasn't built like you. So it was…anticlimactic."

Regan smiled. All righty, then. His ego had been stroked, but not his impatient cock. It wanted to move. "Tell me if this is okay." He drew back and slid forward again.

"Outstanding. More of that."

"How about this?" He initiated a steady rhythm.

"Oh, *yeah.*"

"Faster?"

"Oh, please, yes."

As he picked up the pace, she began to pant and urge him on. He didn't need much urging. His thighs slapped against hers in a frantic tempo amplified by bare walls and floors.

"I'm coming! Oh, Regan, I'm coming!"

Her wild cries and the undulation of her hot channel hurled him over the edge. He surged into her with a bellow of surrender. Locked tight against her firm bottom, he shuddered and moaned as his cock kept pumping. It was the most intense orgasm of his life.

Neither of them moved. He knew he should. He'd planned for this to be short and sweet. Timewise it might qualify as short, but no way had it been sweet. Sweet was lollipops and roses, unicorns and rainbows, kittens and puppies. This coupling had been black velvet, bloodred wine and the low wail of a saxophone. This was sex in its most earthy, sensual, primitive form. And he wanted more of it.

While she remained stretched out against the smooth tabletop, she drew in a shaky breath. "Wow. Way to sabotage a work schedule."

He smiled. "Couldn't help it." Then the smile became a chuckle, and the chuckle morphed into a belly laugh.

"That feels very strange, Regan, since you're still… you know…connected to me. It's sort of vibrator-ish."

He laughed harder. "Is it turning you on?"

"It might if I hadn't just had a peak orgasmic experience, but my private parts are currently in a state of shock and awe."

He couldn't seem to stop laughing. She had a way with words, this girl genius. He supposed that went with the high IQ. "Want me to disconnect so you can recover?"

"I may never recover my dignity. Dear Lord. Bent over a dining room table and taken from behind. What next?"

"Is that a question or a challenge?"

"I'll let you decide. But you probably should let me get up before I dislocate something."

"Okay." Reluctantly he started easing away from paradise.

"Wait."

He paused.

"Promise me something first."

"Good timing. I'm in the mood to promise you anything."

"This one's easy. Don't look."

"At what?"

"Me! Bent over the table in this unflattering position!"

"I find it extremely flattering."

"Maybe before, when you were filled with lust, but I doubt you will now. So promise me you'll close your eyes, turn around and head for the bathroom. Okay?"

He hesitated. "That's a lot to ask of a guy who's all about visual stimulation."

"You don't need any more of that. We have work to do. Promise you'll close your eyes?"

"Sure. I'll close my eyes." He hadn't said when.

"Good. By the time you get back, I'll be presentable."

"All right." He reluctantly backed away. But he sure as hell looked his fill before he left. He could talk until he was blue in the face and never convince her that men enjoyed different visuals from women.

Oh, yeah. He wasn't about to miss that. Surely there wasn't a prettier sight than her freckled bottom, so rosy from the incredible sex they'd just enjoyed. Below that, peeking out seductively, were the moist pink folds of her sex, still swollen with arousal. Any man would remember that sight for the rest of his life. And he was no exception.

LILY SUSPECTED REGAN hadn't honored her request not to look. Her first clue was his soft hum of appreciation after he'd slid out of her. Her second clue was his heartfelt sigh as he walked away. Her third clue was when he started whistling in the bathroom.

He was one happy guy, and come to think of it, she was one happy woman. Too bad he'd shot the timetable all to hell. But once she'd peeled herself off the table, pulled up her pants and walked slightly bowlegged into the kitchen, she was astounded to discover that they weren't so far off schedule, after all. Who would have thought you could pack so much pleasure into so little time?

And oh, the pleasure. She'd never considered herself a hedonist, but a man like Regan could make her reconsider her position. That cowboy knew how to ride. In any position.

Even better, he had the equipment to take that ride to the next level. She'd never been so thoroughly massaged, inside and out. She'd told him that she couldn't be aroused again so soon after such an all-encompassing episode. Apparently that wasn't true, because as she stood in the kitchen, she wanted him again.

Speak of the devil. In he walked, looking fresh as a daisy with his shirt buttoned and tucked into his jeans.

No one would ever know what he'd recently been doing at the dining table. "Ready to do some horse training?"

But anybody who looked at her would guess she'd been had, thoroughly and with gusto. She gazed at him. "You know how women are always saying that guys have it easy when it comes to peeing in the woods?"

"Do they say that?"

"Trust me, they do. Because it's true, if you think about it."

"I suppose it's true. But how does this apply to our current situation? If you're proposing a hike in the woods, or a campout, I don't think that's in the cards. We have too many responsibilities."

He was cute. She had to give him that. "I was merely making the point that men also have it easier when they have sex. Everything's sort of contained in one place, and once they zip up again, they're golden. Women, on the other hand, tend to feel sort of squishy and in need of a hot shower afterward."

His dark gaze was gentle. "By all means take a hot shower, Lily. Meet me down at the corral whenever you're ready."

"I didn't want to wuss out on you."

He smiled. "You aren't wussing. I'm the one who convinced you we had time for sex, remember? You wanted to get right to work."

"And boy, did I hold on to my resolve. Did you notice how tough I was? You really had to labor at changing my mind about having sex. It took at least five seconds."

He closed the gap between them and combed her hair back from her face. "I love that about you. You want me and you don't care if I know it."

"I used to care. At first I did everything I could to hide my reaction to you."

"But the important thing is that you don't hide anything from me now."

"No, I depend on your chivalrous nature not to look at things I'd rather you didn't see." She batted her eyelashes at him, daring him to confess.

"I looked."

"Hell, I know you did! I could tell! I hate thinking that you'll carry that picture around in your head for God knows how long."

"I'll remember it forever."

She groaned. "Great. Etched in Regan O'Connelli's brain forever—Lily King's freckled fanny and her recently enjoyed feminine parts. Lovely."

"They were. Both enjoyed and lovely." He stroked her scalp with his fingertips. "If I let myself dwell on the image too long, I'll drag you into the bedroom, after all."

She tamped down her immediate response to that. If she let him know that she still wanted him, too, they would never get to the training. "We have to exercise some control."

He gazed into her eyes. "I know that. I'm not losing sight of what we have to accomplish for the sake of those horses out there."

"Good. Neither am I."

"So we'll go work for a few hours. But eventually we'll have to give up, because the corral isn't lighted."

"Should I consider that?"

"Not at this point. Installing lighting would be a major disruption. The lines should be underground, so you'd have all kinds of equipment in here. I doubt a construction crew would be able to finish the project in time to do us any good."

"So when it's dark, we're done?"

He smiled. "With the horse training, yes. I'll bet we can find some other projects to occupy our time."

"I don't know what's left on the list. Oral sex, check. Missionary position, check. Doggy style, check."

Heat flickered in his dark eyes. "I'm sure we can come up with a few other variations. You're the brainy one. Set your mind to it."

"Not a good idea. I can't be thinking about sex with you and learning to train horses at the same time. In case you haven't noticed, we're not too good at multi-tasking."

"Then we'll have to explore the options together, won't we?" His gaze dropped to her mouth. "We'll have several hours to do that tonight. I'm sure we can think of some way to entertain ourselves."

"You're a naughty boy, Regan O'Connelli. You know perfectly well I won't be able to forget about sex now. If I'm not effective with the horses, it's your fault."

"You'll be effective with the horses." He dropped a quick kiss on her lips. "Compartmentalize. Horses for the next two hours. Sex after that. Now go take your shower, and think of me while hot water is streaming over your amazing, responsive body. Imagine my hands rubbing your—"

"Stop it!" Laughing, she pushed him away. "Go out to the barn, and *don't* think of me in the shower. It could be dangerous."

"You've got that right." He winked at her. "Don't do anything in that shower that I wouldn't do." Plucking his hat from the counter, he settled it on his head before sauntering out the back door.

Lily found the willpower not to call him back by reminding herself how much the horses needed his help. Yes, she also had to learn how to work with them, but this week the burden of the training would fall on him because he was more experienced and therefore more efficient. If she didn't make it out to the corral for another fifteen minutes, the world wouldn't come to an end.

Normally fifteen minutes was more than enough time for her to take a hot shower. But Regan had awakened a more sensual Lily, a Lily who might just decide to grab a little personal enjoyment while she was in the shower. He'd warned her not to do anything he wouldn't do, which left lots of room to maneuver.

13

REGAN HAD PLENTY of practice at compartmentalizing. He'd used the technique to wall off thoughts about Jeannette while he'd taken the necessary steps to leave Virginia and relocate in Wyoming. But that wall was developing some serious cracks.

As he walked to the barn to pick up a lead rope, Lily was on his mind for obvious reasons, but Jeannette was there, too. After such explosive sex with Lily, he had to face the truth. He and Jeannette had never had that kind of chemistry. Sure, they'd enjoyed the experience. He had some good memories of sex with her. But none of them compared with today's total sensual immersion.

He thought back over the last couple of months he'd spent with his ex-fiancée and reluctantly admitted he'd let their sex life grow stale. He'd planned to spice things up after discovering that he wouldn't be spending Christmas Eve delivering a valuable foal, after all, but that had been an afterthought. Too little, too late. Jeannette very well could have felt neglected and unappreciated. He hadn't wanted to accept any blame for what had happened, but he might want to rethink that position.

He began to remember little things—the sexy nightgown that he'd barely noticed because he'd been exhausted from an all-night vigil with a sick thoroughbred. The candlelight dinner he'd missed when a high-earning stud ate some moldy grain and almost died.

Jeannette had assured him she understood, and he'd believed her. After all, she'd been raised in the world of thoroughbred racing and he'd become the vet of choice for her parents' stable as well as others in their exclusive circle.

But he should have found a way to make it up to her for those little disappointments. He could have been much better at letting her know that he cared. He *had* cared, but in a low-key, comfortable, take-her-for-granted kind of way. Ugh. No wonder she'd been tempted by Drake.

That didn't excuse Drake, though. Regan wasn't cutting that guy any slack. He'd moved in on his best friend's fiancée, and a friend just didn't do that. They'd all known each other since freshman year in college, for God's sake. He and Drake had decided within weeks of meeting in a biology class that someday they'd open a clinic together in Virginia and specialize in thoroughbreds.

Drake had introduced Regan to Jeannette that first semester, too, and the three of them had been inseparable. If she'd cheated with someone else, *anyone* else, Regan wouldn't have reacted with such fury. He'd thought he could trust the guy with his life, but he hadn't even been able to trust him with the woman Regan had planned to marry.

A horse nickered, pulling him out of his dark thoughts. He found himself standing in the barn, fists clenched and jaw tight, wondering what he'd come down there for. Oh, yeah. A lead rope so he could catch himself a horse to train. Might as well grab two ropes and get both horses in the corral at once.

The barn was empty except for Sally, who was the one who'd called to him from her stall at the far end. She probably hoped he'd let her out so she could continue snacking on Lily's house. "Sorry, old girl. You're in a time-out for now."

A rope looped over each shoulder, he headed out of the barn into the sunlight. His shades were clipped to the visor in his truck, and he'd decided to leave them there. Lily thought they were a sign of his secret anguish, so he'd be damned if he'd keep wearing them when she was around.

He didn't want to, anyway. They interfered with his full appreciation of Lily walking through sunbeams, her hair glowing like fire. Damn, wasn't that poetic? She had that effect on him, inspiring him to think in ways that were totally new to him. He'd never had thoughts like that about Jeannette, and he realized now that a guy should be entranced by the woman he intended to spend his life with.

Bottom line, he hadn't loved Jeannette the way he should have, considering the big step they'd been about to take. He hoped she'd find someone who would love her like that. It felt good to wish her well. Thanks to Lily, he could finally do that.

As he walked the property, he evaluated which two horses should come back to the corral with him. Then he noticed Rex standing on a small rise, head up, mane and tail fluttering in the breeze. Okay, that one. He was one of the troublemakers, which meant he might require more effort, but he would show well in the corral. Getting him adopted would eliminate one of Lily's biggest headaches.

Instead of approaching the big palomino, Regan relaxed his posture and waited to see if Rex would come to him. They'd established a tentative bond yesterday. Regan visualized the horse walking right up to him.

Rex looked over at Regan and tossed his head. Then he posed. Regan couldn't describe it any other way, and it made him chuckle. Rex stood with his chest out and his head high, as if to showcase how truly magnificent he was. Regan wasn't sure how long this demonstration might last, so he tried a low whistle, just to see if Rex might have been trained to respond to that.

Rex whinnied exactly as a movie horse might have been taught to do, and walked straight over to Regan. Then he began nosing Regan's pockets for a snack.

"Sorry, no treats." Regan clipped the lead rope on the palomino's halter and started walking back to the corral. Maybe he'd pick up another horse along the way. "Something tells me that whoever brought you in wasn't your first owner. You've been spoiled by more than one person, haven't you, Rex?"

The horse snorted.

"Yeah, thought so." Regan glanced back over his shoulder, and sure enough, several horses had fallen into line behind Rex. Regan would have his pick of another animal to train.

By the time Lily arrived at the corral, Regan was making good progress with Rex. A big bay named Molasses was tied outside the corral waiting his turn. The rest of the horses had drifted away, apparently bored by the proceedings.

Regan spared a quick glance at Lily, who'd left her hair loose around her shoulders. He'd like to believe that was for his benefit. She'd also added a Western hat, which was wise considering her fair skin. She looked darned cute in it, too. After allowing himself one potent image of her red hair spread out on a white pillowcase, he shut down that avenue of thought and concentrated on Rex.

"What can I do?"

"How about untying Molasses and leading him around a bit? See how he does on the lead, unless you already know."

"I don't. Because I never cared where they wandered, I had no reason to put a lead rope on any of them."

"Then finding out how he leads would be a good thing. Holler if you need any help." He figured it would be a good exercise for Lily, too. "By the way, have you ridden any of them?"

"Nope."

"I never thought to ask—do you ride?"

She shrugged. "I rode my friends' horses every so often when I was a kid, but I wouldn't say I'm really confident. That's probably why I didn't think to ride any of these guys, especially being out here alone."

"That's okay, but we should know whether they can be ridden before we adopt them out. Did the people who dropped them off mention whether they were good saddle horses or not?"

"Uh, no. I'm embarrassed about how little information I asked for. I need some sort of intake form, I guess."

She should have created such a form early on, but that was water under the bridge. "Don't worry about it. You have a couple of saddles in the barn we can use. After I've worked with Rex and Molasses for a while, we can saddle them up and take them out."

"You mean go riding?"

"Sure." He had a sudden thought. "Unless you're too tender."

She laughed. "Not yet. But if I'm going to be riding horses this week, then maybe we should refrain from—"

"Sorry. Not acceptable. I'll ride the horses."

That made her laugh even more. "My, my. I can tell where your priorities are."

"As if you had any doubt."

"Let's see how it goes. Maybe I can do both. As for this afternoon, I'd love to take a ride with you, assuming neither of these boys is a bucking bronco."

"I'll make sure of that before I let you get on one."

"I'd appreciate that. Okay, I'm off for a walk with Molasses. I won't go far, in case I need your help."

"Good idea." He hoped she'd get along fine with Molasses, so he wouldn't be required to come to her rescue. That would bode well for both woman and horse. But he was a typical guy, after all, and he'd discovered that being a woman's white knight was pretty damned cool.

LILY DIDN'T HAVE a single problem with Molasses. She couldn't decide if he walked quietly behind her at a respectful distance because he was well trained, or if he was responding to her more assertive attitude. She followed the tips Regan had taught her earlier that day with Sally and simply assumed Molasses would do what was expected of him.

Fortunately for both of them, he did. When Molasses had his turn in the corral with Regan, he was a model horse, so maybe his behavior had nothing to do with her new attitude.

"I have a feeling we'll be able to take that ride," Regan said as he came through the gate leading Molasses. "I had no trouble with this boy."

"Me, either." Lily untied Rex and walked beside Regan as they all headed toward the barn. "I guess that's because he's just a good horse."

"Not necessarily. It might be that he recognizes you mean business."

"I really have changed my attitude. Sally chewing on the windowsill was the last straw."

"That bothered you more than the porch railing?"

"You betcha it did! Replacing and repainting that railing would have been work, but doable. Replacing a windowsill, especially for an older, double-hung window like that one, would have been a pain in the neck."

"Yep." He glanced over at her and smiled. "I'm glad you saw the light."

"I did. I'm a changed woman."

"Hey, let's not get carried away. I like you fine the way you are."

"I was too permissive. I can't be that way anymore."

"With the *animals*. But I love it when you're permissive with me."

Her body began to hum. "Way to sidetrack me, O'Connelli. I was completely focused on this horse-training exercise until you said *that*."

"You were? Honestly?"

"Mostly. A girl has to sneak a peek now and then."

"So does a guy. Especially when he's training a mellow horse like Molasses."

"Mmm." She began replaying their bedroom and dining activities, and her panties were suddenly no longer so dry. "Out of curiosity, how long a ride were you planning on?"

"Long enough to take us out to the back of your property."

"Okay. That's not very far."

"Just far enough."

"I suppose you don't need a cross-country trek to find out if they'll behave themselves with a person on their back."

"No, I don't. And there's a nice tree out there."

She couldn't imagine what the tree had to do with the riding test. "Are you into trees?"

"Sure."

"So do you want me to ride Molasses, since he seems like such an easy horse?"

"I'll probably have you ride Rex. I'm more confident of his behavior now that we've worked together twice. But let's see how they react to being saddled before we decide."

Lily stepped back and let Regan saddle both horses, in case either of them kicked up a fuss. They didn't, but she knew Regan was visualizing that they'd stand there without protest, so that's what they did. She was becoming a fan of assumed consent.

"I'll mount Rex first," Regan said. "If he reacts okay to that, you can get on him."

"I'm hoping I'll remember how to do this."

"I'm sure you will." Regan tightened the cinch on Rex's saddle. He talked to the palomino in that same low, calming voice that seemed so effective. Then he rubbed the horse's shoulder and scratched under his mane before leaning against the saddle for a couple of seconds.

Finally he swung up into the saddle. Rex turned to look at who was on his back. "Just me," Regan said. As if satisfied with that, Rex faced forward again.

"So far, so good." Lily was trying not to think sexy thoughts, but Regan looked mighty fine sitting on a flashy horse. When he'd swung into the saddle with that easy confidence of his, her heart rate had sped up.

Regan dismounted. "He'll be okay. Let me test Molasses before you climb aboard Rex, though."

"Okay." She stood back as he repeated the routine with the bay gelding. Turned out he looked equally good there. Regan was impressive no matter what he was doing, but when he mounted a horse—oh, baby. That ramped up his sexiness quotient by about a thousand percent.

"Molasses is fine, too." He swung down again. "Go on and get up on Rex so I can adjust your stirrups."

She climbed up on the horse and tested the stirrups. Definitely too long. She sat astride the saddle breathing in the scent of warm leather and warm man as Regan worked on the stirrups, his face inches from her thigh. "I'm having improper thoughts," she murmured.

"Good. So am I." He moved back. "Try those out."

She stood in the stirrups. "Perfect."

He glanced up at her. "Yes, ma'am, you are."

Her breath caught at the warmth in his eyes. Desire was there, but something more, something tender and sweet. "I'm far from perfect."

"Not too far." He gave her a crooked grin. "At least that's my totally unbiased opinion." He squeezed her thigh. "Visualize this horse doing everything you ask him to."

"I will." She wondered if the technique would work on Regan. Then again, she really didn't need it. Judging from the way he'd just looked at her, he'd gladly do everything she asked him to, especially when they were both naked.

Now there was an arousing thought, as if she needed one. As they walked the horses away from the barn, she discovered that riding as an adult was a far more sensual experience than she remembered from when she was a kid. Or maybe she wouldn't have noticed the erotic nature of sitting astride a powerful animal if she hadn't recently had amazing sex with the man riding along next to her.

He turned his head and caught her staring at him. "You doing okay, pretty lady?"

"Fine."

"Be sure and tell me if anything is making you uncomfortable."

She watched as his hips moved in rhythm with the bay gelding. Meanwhile she dealt with the soft friction provided by a denim seam as it rocked against the leather saddle. By the end of this outing, she would be more than ready for a different kind of ride. "Define *uncomfortable*."

"Painful."

"Then I'm good." She faced forward, because she simply couldn't continue to look at him without wanting to have him six ways to Sunday.

"I think we have a couple of trained saddle horses here. I can tell that to people with confidence on Saturday. They're also good-looking, which never hurts.

Somebody will see that showy palomino and fall in love, I'll bet. Molasses isn't as eye-catching, but he has good lines."

"You aren't worried about Rex's aggressive behavior yesterday?"

"We need to ask a lot of questions about the home he'll be going to. He'll want to be the herd leader, and he requires his own stall. But if they understand that and they're firm with him, I think it'll work out."

"I hope so." The conversation distracted her a little, but her gaze kept wandering to his tight buns cupped lovingly by the saddle. When her lust threatened to get the best of her, she faced forward again. Sure enough, they were headed for that tree he seemed so crazy about. "If someone adopted Rex, it would ease my mind about fights breaking out."

"That's my thought. We'll concentrate on him. But I plan to train Strawberry, next. If both of them left, you'd be much better off."

"I would." As they drew closer to the tree, she noticed that it had a little patch of grass under it. The horses must have been grazing there in the shade, because it looked as if someone had mowed it. "Nice little spot there."

"It is. Nicer than I expected, even. How about stopping for a minute? We can find out how the horses behave if we tie them to that low branch on the far side."

"Fine with me." She was ready to take a break from constant stimulation to her private parts augmented by the hot cowboy riding almost within touching distance.

Regan swung down from his horse. "Beautiful view from out here. I love the way the shadows fall on the Tetons this time of day."

"Do you miss Virginia?" It was as much as she dared ask. Of course he had some bad memories connected to the place, but he'd lived there for several years, both when he attended college and after he opened a clinic with his friend Drake. Wyoming's rugged terrain was nothing like the manicured pastures and wooded hills of Virginia.

"No, I don't." He walked Molasses over to the low branch on the far side of the tree. "Getting accepted into the University of Virginia gave me an ego boost, and I made some…some good friends there. I stayed for the people more than the landscape, although it's pretty."

She heard the catch in his voice and knew he had to be thinking of the two people who'd betrayed him. "I'm sorry it didn't work out for you there." She walked Rex over to where Molasses was tied and secured her horse's reins to the same branch.

"I'm not. Not anymore." The emotion edging his words made his meaning clear.

As she met his gaze and saw the frank appreciation there, her chest grew tight. If she was his rebound girl, apparently she'd succeeded in mending his broken heart. She told herself not to worry that this was the beginning of the end. Just because she'd had a rotten experience once before—when the guy had recovered from a breakup and then left her—didn't mean it would happen again.

"Let's go sit on the grass for a minute." He held out his hand.

She took it, and her heart squeezed. They were holding hands, just like in his vision of cliff diving. She could fall for this man. She might already be falling. If that was a mistake, she didn't know how to undo it.

He led her over to the little patch of grass before releasing her hand. "Pick your spot."

She chose one dappled with shade and sat down cross-legged. Taking off her hat, she finger-combed her hair and lifted it off the back of her neck. He remained standing, and she looked up at him. From this angle, she had a fine view of his excellent and talented package. She'd take that view over the Tetons any day. "Aren't you going to sit down?"

"Yeah. I just like watching you." Pushing back his hat with his thumb, he settled down facing her so their knees bumped. "And I like touching you and kissing you and feeling you come when I'm deep inside you."

She quivered as heat surged through her. "How you talk, cowboy."

"I like it when you blush." His smile crinkled the corners of his eyes. "It makes your freckles stand out."

"You're about to make me vain about those freckles."

"You should be." Reaching over, he threaded his fingers through her hair. "I just want you to know that you're an amazing woman." He rubbed a strand of her hair between his fingers. "Until I met you… Correction, until you invited me into your bedroom to handle your problem—"

"Cheesy, wasn't it?"

"Nope. Fun. Like you." He held her gaze. "I had no idea what I was missing, Lily. I never dreamed I could want a woman this much. I lived in a colorless world with no real passion. You inspire me to be different."

She wanted him so much she could barely breathe. "You inspire me, too."

"When I suggested riding out here, I was thinking

we could have some outdoor sex, since we hadn't done that yet."

"Oh." Surprisingly, she hadn't considered that, but now that he'd told her, she began to ache in predictable places. She hoped he hadn't given up on the idea.

"I pictured it as another quick romp to tide us over until after we'd fed the animals and had more time to ourselves."

"Sounds good to me."

"Now that we're here, it doesn't sound so good to me."

"It doesn't?" She certainly hadn't expected to hear that. Canceling her ticket on the orgasm train wouldn't be easy. Maybe she should just tackle him. "Why not?"

"Because I don't want it to be quick. I want it to be slow and sweet."

"Oh!" Apparently they were back in business. Goody.

"I want you stretched out naked in this fragrant grass while I kiss every freckle on your silky skin. Then I want to slide into you, over and over, and tell you how beautiful you are while I make you come."

"Oh." If he kept talking like that, she might spontaneously combust without benefit of penis.

"What I want, Lily King, is to make love to you."

"Ohhhh." For the second time in two days, she nearly swooned.

14

REGAN HAD CHOSEN his words carefully when he'd announced that he wanted to make love to Lily. Earlier today they'd had sex, and maybe they'd just have sex again in the future. But this time was about gratitude. Six months ago he hadn't felt particularly fortunate. Today he'd realized he was the luckiest guy in the world.

Lily had shown him that. He wanted to show her what she meant to him, and for that, they needed to make love. He didn't confuse it with being *in* love. They hadn't known each other long enough for that to happen. But that didn't mean they couldn't *make* love. Besides, who knew? Maybe one day soon they would discover that they'd fallen, and fallen hard.

They undressed each other with care, taking time to lay their clothes in a neat pile. They took even more time to kiss and nuzzle each other along the way. When Lily finally lay back on the cool grass, Regan's cock felt as if it was made of tempered steel. He'd clenched his jaw as he'd rolled on the condom. If he wasn't careful, he could come just by looking at her lying there.

Yet he wanted to look at her and burn her image into

his memory. So he knelt beside her, rigid cock notwith-standing, and memorized the picture she made. Green was definitely her color. The soft grass set her off like a jewel nestled in velvet, highlighting her fiery hair and pale skin dusted with cinnamon and nutmeg.

A breeze ruffled the leaves over her head, and shad-ows danced over her body. She seemed one with nature, a sensual female aroused and ready to be taken by a lustful male. And he was that male...for now.

An emotion stirred deep in his chest, an unfamiliar one. It felt...ancient. It had no place here, and he shoved it away, but still he heard it whisper. *Mine.*

Reaching up, she stroked his cheek. "Such a fierce expression you have."

"Do I?" He met her clear-eyed gaze. He must have been carried away by the setting. "I was concentrating while I counted all your freckles. I don't want to miss any of them when I start the kissing part."

She smiled. "We'll be here all night."

"Maybe." Leaning down, he kissed a sweet little freckle on her breast. "One." Then another. "Two."

She laughed as he kept kissing and counting, but then he paused and drew a nipple into his mouth. She didn't laugh then. She moaned and held his head to her breast, her fingertips pressing into his scalp.

Her urgency fed into that ancient voice telling him to claim her. No, he would not. But he abandoned freckle-counting for the more primitive pleasures of nibbling and licking her breasts while he caressed her damp thighs and sought out the slick heat waiting for him.

She moaned again and arched upward, inviting him deeper. Capturing her mouth to muffle her cries, he stroked her until she came, bathing his fingers in her juices. As she lay panting beside him, he trailed his hand up her flushed body and anointed her lips. Then he leaned over and kissed her.

The heady taste sipped from her mouth made him a little crazy. He wanted, *needed* more. Kissing his way back along the damp trail he'd made with his fingers, he moved between her thighs. The scent of crushed grass and fragrant earth mingled with the aroma of sex as he settled his mouth against her heat.

With the first lap of his tongue she sighed and opened wider, offering herself so completely that his breath caught. *Mine.* He feasted until her whimpering cries told him she was close.

Sliding slowly up her restless body, he effortlessly buried his cock in her drenched channel. He felt the quiver, knew she was almost there. "Wait," he murmured. "Wait for me."

She gulped. "Okay."

When he was locked in tight, he braced himself on his forearms and gazed down at her.

She looked right back at him, her eyes dark with passion, her red hair spread out over the grass like tongues of flame.

He was stunned by the force of his desire for her. "It's never been like this for me."

"Me, either."

That helped, knowing she'd been blindsided, too. "I don't know what's going to happen."

She smiled at that. "I do. We're both going to come."

"Yeah." He appreciated any attempt to lighten the mood, because wow, this was intense. "And we can't be loud and scare the horses."

"I know." She stroked his back and pressed her fingers into his backside. "Ready for some cliff diving?"

"Yes." And he began to thrust, holding her gaze as the rhythm escalated, watching her eyes. He saw arousal there, but he also saw wonder, and maybe just a touch of fear. His expression probably told the same story.

Faster, now…almost there…

She gasped. "Now."

"Yes…" He gulped for air. "Jump." He kissed her and swallowed her cries as her climax rolled over his cock. Then he broke away to drag in a breath, clenched his jaw and came in a furious rush that left him reeling. He felt the shock of it from his scalp to his toes.

Breathing hard, he closed his eyes and somehow managed not to fall on her. When at last he felt recovered enough to open them, he discovered that she'd closed hers, too. She appeared suddenly more vulnerable lying there in the grass, her cheeks blushing from a recent climax and her mouth red from his kisses. As if waiting for this moment, the ancient whisper sounded again. *Mine.*

But she wasn't his or any man's. She was her own person, and yet…if she was into this as much as he was, she was trusting him not to hurt her as that other bastard had. She'd said she didn't care if this was a rebound relationship, but he wasn't sure he believed that.

God, he hoped he hadn't used her to get over Jeannette. A rush of protectiveness made him vow that he wouldn't let anyone hurt her. And that included him.

IN THE NEXT few days, Lily worked harder and enjoyed more great sex than she'd ever had in her entire life. She also couldn't remember being happier. She and Regan were creating a practical rescue operation at Peaceful Kingdom, and that was extremely satisfying. And bonus, so was the sex.

Somehow they managed to get the work done and still have time to fool around. Often they had to get creative, such as when they made quiet but highly orgasmic love on a hay bale while the horses ate breakfast. They'd done that twice.

Lily found herself walking around with a song in her heart and a smile on her face. She'd always been a cheerful person, but these days it seemed as if nothing would get her down. She was in high spirits when Nick and Lester showed up late Thursday afternoon to help work with the horses.

Having someone around felt a little strange after all the private time she'd had with Regan. But on Friday night everyone would descend to help set up, so in effect, the isolation she and Regan had enjoyed was nearly over. Lester, it turned out, had a special affinity with horses and planned to be a trainer some day. So Regan invited him out to the newly constructed pasture to help pick out two animals they'd train until the corral became too dark. That left Nick and Lily free to lean on the corral and discuss the progress that had been made so far.

"Everything's in place," Nick said. "Your fliers have been distributed. Some basic food's been ordered, which Mary Lou will be in charge of on Saturday. Dominique will be here to take pictures, and we managed to nix the jumping castle and the cotton candy machine."

"I'm just as glad. I know Tyler was worried about entertaining the kids, but I'm afraid a jumping castle would involve a lot of noise that might bother the horses."

"She was going to set it up quite a ways from the corral, but still, I agree. It's expensive and potentially disruptive. Tyler's hired someone who does face painting, and she's organized an activity table for the kids with coloring and a few simple crafts."

"Did she decide to have a band?" Lily had been a little worried about that possibility.

"After much discussion, not doing it."

"That's a relief. I know some barns have music piped in, but since I don't do that, I'm afraid a band might be another distraction. Regan and I have enough on our hands getting the horses ready for all that activity without adding a potential hazard."

"Which brings me to another point. You two have done a terrific job this week. The porch railing's fixed, the flower beds are replanted and the new sign is gorgeous."

"Thanks." Lily beamed at the compliment. The sign read Peaceful Kingdom Equine Rescue, and it had turned out beautifully. "I was lucky to find somebody local who could create that sign on short notice. Regan and I have worked hard."

"I can tell. And hanging out with him must suit you," Nick said. "I've never seen you looking so…settled."

That startled her. "What do you mean by *settled?*"

"Don't take this wrong, but I've always viewed you as a tropical bird about to take flight."

"And now I look like what? A roosting chicken?"

Nick laughed. "I was thinking more like a turtle dove."

"Wait a minute." She panicked at the idea that her feelings for Regan were that obvious. "Don't go making any assumptions."

"What assumptions? You two like each other and you're both single. I'm happy for you."

"You haven't said anything like that to Regan, I hope." She would die of mortification if he had.

"No, I haven't, so don't get your undies in a bunch. He's been tearing in and out of the office all week like a madman so he can take care of his clients and help you out here. We've barely said two words to each other."

"That's a relief."

"But when I have seen him, he always had a smile on his face. I can't say that's been the case prior to his moving in here. So I figure you've been good for him, too."

"I hope so, but please don't jump to conclusions." She broke out in a cold sweat at the thought of Nick pushing Regan into an admission of his feelings for her one way or the other. Neither of them had taken that step, and maybe they never would.

"Okay, but tomorrow night you'll have a whole mob of people who are liable to jump to conclusions. You might want to decide how to handle that."

That was a scary thought. She sent him a pleading glance. "Could you caution everyone not to ask any leading questions? We're at an uncertain stage right now, and I don't want him to feel pressured."

"I can say something, but there's no way I can control that bunch. Regan knows what they're like. Have a talk with him. Come up with your standard responses."

"Okay, I will." She cleared her throat. "I can't deny that Regan and I are having a little fun, but I think it would be foolish of me or anyone to take his interest too seriously. He just broke up with his fiancée. He's not ready for another relationship."

"Could've fooled me." Nick adjusted the fit of his Stetson. "If anything, he looks happier than you do."

"Well, sure, he looks *happy*. That doesn't mean he's in *love* or anything." That last part had been harder to say than she'd expected.

Nick stared at the Tetons as the afternoon shadows gathered in the canyons. "Mighty pretty view."

"It is." She figured he was buying time as he decided how to approach an obviously delicate subject.

"Look, God knows I'm no expert on this subject, but I think both of you are heading into that kind of emotional territory, at least a little bit. And if you want my advice—"

"Not really."

"You'll keep an open mind," he continued, ignoring her protest.

"Nick, six months isn't long enough. Most people need a year to get over a thing like that."

"Maybe most people do, but don't assume he's most people and don't assume he's not ready. Everybody heals at a different rate. My guess is that Regan's more resilient than most because of his parents."

"His *parents?*" That shocked her.

"That's what I said. Got a banana in your ear?"

"I heard you fine, but judging from what he's told me, he doesn't agree with their lifestyle or their parenting skills."

"He might not, but I've had a few years to observe the O'Connelli crew, and while Seamus and Bianca might have been too permissive, their kids never doubted they were loved. They all have an unshakable belief in their own worth."

Lily thought about Regan's quiet confidence, especially when he was working with the horses. "You may have a point."

"I generally do."

She looked sideways at him and couldn't help laughing at his cocky grin. "I'll bet Dominique has to use a wide-angle lens to get you and your ego into the same frame."

He chuckled. "I'll tell her you said that. She'll love it. She wanted to come over to see you tonight, but she's mounting a new show at the gallery, and that's sucking up all her spare time. Plus, as she pointed out, she's not a horse trainer."

"Neither am I."

"According to Regan, you're better than you think you are, which doesn't surprise me. You have a lot of empathy. I'm glad to see you getting into this. I think it suits you better than whatever IT gigs you had in Silicon Valley. Every time I talked to your folks you'd switched jobs."

"Because I'd get bored."

"Maybe that's because you're more into living creatures than electronic gizmos."

"You think so?" No one had ever said that to her before. "You don't feel like I'm wasting my intelligence on this project?"

"How could you be? In order to make a success of this venture, you'll have to learn to think like a horse, run a business and attract both donors and potential adopters. Isn't that enough of a challenge for you?"

"When you put it that way, yes."

"Who said you were wasting your intelligence?"

She thought back to a phone call she'd had yesterday, one she hadn't mentioned to Regan. "A computer game company in Palo Alto wants me to work for them. I told them I don't want to leave this place, and they said that while I might be able to telecommute from here, they generally discourage it. They've found that having everyone on site interacting with other designers contributes to more innovation."

"Are you considering it?"

"No, of course not." She watched Regan walking back with Lester, small for his age but incredibly likable. Each of them led a horse and both animals looked docile as could be. "Certainly not now, anyway."

Nick took a deep breath and blew it out. "Lily, you're not going to break that guy's heart, are you?"

"No." Longing tugged at her, as it always did when she looked at Regan. "But I'm still not entirely convinced he won't break mine."

15

REGAN WAS GRATEFUL for the Chance clan pitching in. Without them there would be no adoption fair, and Lily desperately needed to find good homes for at least six of the horses under her care. But their Peaceful Kingdom had been invaded late Friday afternoon by a Chance contingent ready to set up for the fair, and Regan knew he wouldn't get to be alone with Lily until late tonight. By then they'd both be too exhausted to make love.

On top of that, they'd agreed to be careful how they interacted with each other to keep gossip to a minimum. She'd told him about Nick's suggestion that they come up with a standard response to any questions. It was *We're just good friends*. Regan didn't think anyone would believe that BS, but he said it, anyway, because apparently that's what Lily wanted.

He was a little irritated that she didn't want to go public with their relationship. What was wrong with letting close friends and family know they were involved? They suspected it, anyway, so why be coy? But Lily insisted on a party line, so he was doing as she asked, because in the end, he'd do just about anything that woman asked.

They'd been on a deadline situation this past week, but once they got successfully past the adoption fair, he needed to have a heart-to-heart with her. Technically he'd have no more excuse to live in her house. Oh, yeah, and that was the other thing. He'd had to move all his stuff to the guest room and pretend he was sleeping there. Lame.

Anyway, he'd go along until after the fair, and then he'd flat out ask her how she felt about him. Would she still want him around when she no longer needed him to help her with the animals? Now that she had a paddock, a chicken coop and a pigpen, she could handle her menagerie a lot easier. Once a few horses went out the door, it would be a piece of cake for a woman of her abilities.

So then what? They each needed to lay their cards on the table. He wanted to stay. He thought they had something going and he wanted to find out where it would take them. She might feel differently. Thinking about having that talk made him nervous as hell, but it had to be done.

Right now, though, he didn't have much time to contemplate the next step in their relationship. He was too busy helping set up bleachers next to the corral, a canopy for Mary Lou's refreshment stand and another canopy for the kids' activity center. Jack, Nick and Gabe were in the barn grooming the horses so they'd shine like new pennies. Although they'd settled on showcasing only ten of the twenty-one, Jack had insisted that every horse look tip-top to enhance the image of the place. He had a point.

Regan was so busy moving from one job to the next that it was a wonder he even heard his phone. But when he did, he considered not answering. He knew that ring. He'd assigned it to the caller several years ago and had never bothered to change it or delete the number from his contacts.

He couldn't just let it go to voice mail. At the last minute, he punched the button and walked over to a darkened spot in the yard, away from all the action. "What?"

"Hey, Regan." Drake's voice sounded strained. "I wasn't sure you'd pick up."

"I almost didn't."

Drake didn't respond at first. "I get that," he said at last. "The thing is, I'm here."

"Here?" Regan's grip tightened on the phone and he glanced toward the gate as if expecting Drake to come walking through it. "What do you mean, *here?*"

"In Jackson Hole. Not too far from that little town you always talked about, Shoshone."

"What the hell are you doing in Jackson Hole?"

"Two things. I needed some time to think, and I needed to see you."

"Can't imagine why you need to see me." The anger he thought he'd tucked away came boiling to the surface. "We have nothing to discuss."

"You said that six months ago, too. You may have nothing to say to me, but I have plenty to say to you. I'd like that opportunity, Regan. For old time's sake."

"Old time's sake?" He realized he'd gotten loud, and he walked farther into the shadows and lowered his voice. His heart was pounding like a snare drum. "I can't believe you can say such a thing. Old time's sake?

You don't give a shit about old times, Drake. Don't pretend like you do."

More silence, followed by a sigh. "Okay, forget about that. Don't agree to talk with me because of our former friendship. I suppose that's not important. Something else is, though. You're still furious with me. I can hear it in your voice."

"What if I am? That's my business."

"True. But this situation isn't good for either of us. We're both festering, Regan. You're a doctor. You know wounds like this have to be lanced. Let's get together and take care of that. If we end up beating each other to a bloody pulp, so be it. At least we'll get it out, drain off the bad stuff."

While a part of him longed to get into a fistfight with Drake, he'd have to actually be in the same room with the guy to make that happen. He had no wish to do that. "Sorry. You've caught me at a bad time. I'm too busy to play your silly reindeer games."

"That's good, at least. It's good to be busy."

"Yes, it is. Now, if you'll excuse me, I have to get back to what I was doing."

"Yeah, okay. But if you change your mind, I'm going to be here for a couple of months."

"A couple of *months?*" In spite of not wanting to prolong the conversation, Regan couldn't resist asking about that. "It's the middle of the damned thoroughbred racing season! How can you afford to be out here instead of back at the clinic? Or even more to the point, how can you leave your parents and their cronies in the lurch like that?"

"I have someone covering for me. If he gets overwhelmed, there are plenty of vets in the area who will be glad to have the business."

Regan wasn't sure he'd heard right. "You don't care if your parents are pissed? You don't care if your business goes down the tubes because you needed a long vacation?" That wasn't the Drake Brewster he knew.

"No, I don't. Those things aren't a priority right now. I have two goals—getting my head out of my ass and talking things out with you. Since the first one will probably take at least two months, I thought I'd make a start on achieving the second one."

"Good luck with that. I have no interest in seeing you."

"Just think about it. I know you, Regan, and you *will* think about it. The cabin where I'm staying is just outside the boundaries of the Last Chance Ranch."

"How the hell did you know to go there?"

"That's where you had me forward your mail, Regan. The cabin's owner said the Chance family knows where the place is, so they can direct you if you decide to pay me a visit."

"I won't."

"Your choice."

"You bet it is. Goodbye, Drake." He disconnected the call and stood in the darkness, adrenaline pumping through his system. Damn Drake Brewster to hell and back. Regan began to pace in a tight circle, keeping to the shadows.

This *sucked.* Right when he was starting to mellow out and enjoy life again, specifically life with Lily King, and forget about that nasty chapter in his past, here was Drake to remind him of it. Worse yet, the guy intended to stay in that little cabin for two friggin' *months.*

Sure as anything, Regan would run into him at the Shoshone Diner, or at the ice-cream parlor, or...wait. The most likely place would be Spirits and Spurs. Shit! Now Regan wouldn't be able to go in for a beer without worrying about Brewster riding a bar stool and polluting the atmosphere by his very presence.

Regan wanted him gone, but it was a free country. He couldn't make Drake leave. His only recourse was to convince him, one way or another. And that meant going over to that blasted cabin. Damn it!

"Regan?"

He turned, and there stood Lily looking worried. No wonder; he'd been pacing and muttering to himself like a crazy man. "What?"

"I came to ask you something, but...you're obviously upset. What's wrong?"

"I..." He took off his hat and scrubbed his fingers through his hair. His head hurt. His whole body hurt. He crammed his hat back on. "Never mind. It'll take too long to explain." With a supreme effort, he dredged up a smile. None of this was Lily's fault. "What's the question?"

She hesitated. "Is this problem something I need to know about?"

"Eventually. Not right this minute. What's up?"

"Dominique's offered to make up a poster showing each horse, just the face, and their name underneath. She can do it tonight, no problem. But should we include the lifers on there? And if so, how should we label them?"

"Not *lifers*." That made him smile for real. This past week he and Lily had started calling the permanent six by that nickname. "Sounds like we're running a prison.

How about calling them permanent residents and the others temporary guests?"

"That works. I'll let her know." She paused. "Sure you can't tell me what's got you so upset?"

"Drake called." Just saying those words made it more real. His chest felt as if someone had wrapped a steel band around it and pulled it tight.

Her eyes widened. "Why?"

"He's here in Jackson Hole. Staying in a little cabin near the Last Chance boundary for two months. He wants to talk."

"Wow." She regarded him silently for a few minutes, her eyes full of compassion. "Well...maybe that's good."

"Good? How can that be good? I came here to get away from the bastard!"

"I know, but...if you could clear the air..."

He stared at her in disbelief. Apparently she hadn't been paying attention. "Sure, why not? Then everything will be fine. We can sit around a campfire, tell jokes and sing 'Kumbaya.'"

"I'm not saying it will be easy, but if he's holding out the olive branch, don't you have an obligation to take it after all you meant to each other?"

"No! I don't have a single obligation when it comes to Drake Brewster!"

She didn't respond to that, but he could tell from her expression that she didn't agree with him. She thought he should make nice with his former best friend, mend the fences and forge a new relationship. Bull. Her advice sounded familiar, though. His parents had counseled him to do the exact same thing the last time he'd talked to them.

"I'm not going to engage in some damned sensitivity session with Drake so that he can feel better about himself, Lily. I have no *obligation* to ease his guilty conscience. He did what he did, and now he can suffer the consequences. End of story."

She seemed about to say something, but then she didn't. "Okay, fine. I'll go tell Dominique how to label the horses." She walked away, clearly disappointed in his reaction.

He wasn't too happy with hers, either, but he shouldn't be surprised. She was the softie, the one who couldn't help but say yes, the one who hadn't been firm with the horses because she hadn't wanted to damage their fragile egos. Naturally she'd want him to smooth things over with Drake. He wasn't about to do that. Not even for her.

THE CHANCE FOLKS left around midnight. Earlier tonight Lily had looked forward to them leaving so she could spend some quality time with Regan. Now the issue of Drake hung between them. She could sweep it under the rug and pretend it didn't matter while they frolicked in her bed, but that wasn't her style.

If she'd been in this relationship only for the sex, she might have considered ignoring Regan's attitude toward Drake. But wonderful as the sex had been all week, the friendship they'd created was even more important to her. And friends didn't let friends go off the rails, at least not without making some attempt to help.

They stood together on the porch waving as the last of the Chance trucks pulled away. Lily felt good about the preparations. The horses were better disciplined, and Peaceful Kingdom looked like an organized rescue operation instead of the helter-skelter project it had been a week ago.

She turned to Regan. "Thank you for all you've done. The adoption fair is going to be awesome."

"It should run smoothly." There was a reserved note in his voice that hadn't been there a few hours ago.

She hated that, but judging from his cautious mood, she couldn't have coaxed him into mindless sex even if she'd thought it was a good idea. They'd become so close in the past week, but they didn't have a firm foundation that would allow them to postpone an important discussion while they blew off steam. The discussion had to come first.

Earlier this evening she'd put on a fleece hoodie to ward off the chill of an early June night. Regan was wearing a denim jacket for the same reason. She decided to take advantage of that and suggest they stay out here and talk. For one thing, the porch was about the only place they hadn't made love. It could be their neutral zone.

"How about sitting on the steps here for a little while before we go in?" She visualized a positive response, the way he'd taught her to do with the horses. She'd discovered sometimes it worked with people, too.

He blew out a breath. "That's probably a good idea. I want to explain a few things."

"Good." She sat down on the top step. "I'm all ears."

He sat next to her but not close enough to touch. That in itself was telling. Usually when they were alone, he couldn't get close enough. "I told you nobody knew the details of that Christmas Eve but the three people involved. I want you to know them, so you'll understand."

"Okay."

Resting his elbows on his knees, he laced his fingers together. She wanted him to reach out and take her hand, but he didn't choose to do that. "Let me give you some quick background. Drake was the first friend I made my freshman year at UV. We did everything together. He introduced me to Jeannette, and then the three of us hung out a lot, sometimes adding whatever girl Drake was dating at the time. He never stayed with any very long."

"Could he have been secretly in love with Jeannette?"

"No."

"You're sure?"

"Yep. And before you ask, she wasn't secretly in love with him, either. We were together a *lot*. I would have picked up on it."

"Guess so." Lily wasn't totally convinced, but she let it go. This wasn't about what she thought.

"After graduation, Drake and I went into practice together. His parents own racehorses and so do many of their friends, including Jeannette's folks. With contacts like that, we couldn't help but succeed. To no one's surprise, Jeannette and I got engaged."

"Right."

Regan cleared his throat and stared into the darkness. "As I said the other day, I've thought about that engagement a lot lately, and I'll admit I wasn't the most attentive guy. I let work interfere too much. In fact, I'd expected to spend that Christmas Eve delivering a foal, but it turned out to be false labor. So I got to go home to Jeannette. Instead of calling to say I was on my way, I decided to surprise her."

Lily's stomach lurched. Poor Regan.

"When I saw Drake's SUV sitting in front of our town house, I figured he'd pulled his usual trick of shopping on Christmas Eve. He's famous for that. I thought he was delivering our last-minute gift."

She put her hand on his arm because she had to touch him. His muscles stiffened, but she kept her hand there. "I'm sorry. So, so sorry."

"I walked in, thinking they'd be in the living room, or maybe back in the kitchen, because Jeannette had promised to make cinnamon rolls for Christmas morning. Then I heard her upstairs. She was…moaning with obvious pleasure."

Lily sucked in a breath and laid her head on his arm. "Horrible."

"They said it was the first time they'd had sex, and the thing is, I believe that's true. But once was all it took for me to realize that I never wanted to see Drake Brewster again."

She squeezed his arm and gazed at his profile, which looked as if it had been carved in granite. "I don't blame you."

His shoulders relaxed a little. "Thank you. I figured if I told you the whole story, you'd understand."

"I do. Oh, Regan, I do. But…"

"But?" He looked squarely at her. "Surely after hearing my side of the story, you're not going to tell me I should meet with him."

"Not for his sake."

"Damn straight! Then why go?"

"For your sake, so you can put this behind you."

"I *have* put it behind me!"

"No, you haven't. If you had, then you wouldn't care if Drake showed up here. But he did, and you're beside yourself. You need to go see him, Regan, and make peace with the situation."

His jaw worked as he stared straight ahead. "You'll be happy to know that I do have to go see him. But I'm only doing it because it's how I'll get him to leave. I won't be going to make peace with the situation. I'll be going to get his ass out of my town." Standing, he walked into the house.

She didn't have to ask if he was moving his things back into her bedroom. She knew the answer. Clutching her stomach, she leaned over and rested her forehead on her knees. The pain of letting herself fall for Regan O'Connelli was about to start.

16

REGAN COUNTED the adoption fair a modest success. They'd adopted out only five horses when he would have preferred six or seven, but two of the five had been Rex and Strawberry. Molasses had also found a good home. That left sixteen horses for twelve stalls, but with the paddock available and the two most assertive geldings gone, it was workable.

He and Nick had finished dismantling the bleachers and strapped them onto the flatbed provided by the Chances. Regan took off his gloves and held out his hand. "Couldn't have done this without you, buddy. You and the rest of the family."

"Glad to. It's a great cause and I want Lily to succeed at this."

"Yeah, me, too." Thoughts of Lily were extremely painful at the moment, but he didn't want Nick to know that. Working with her all day and exchanging only clipped words had been horrible. The past few hours ranked as some of the worst of his life.

"So you think you'll be staying on here? Not that we don't love having you at the ranch, but those boys arrive tomorrow, and the second floor won't exactly be a quiet haven anymore."

Regan had no idea what he was doing at this point. "I have to talk to Lily," he said. "She might be ready to kick me out." He made it sound like a joke.

"I sincerely doubt that." Nick had a speculative gleam in his eyes, though, as if he was catching something bubbling under the surface. "Whatever you decide is fine. Just warning you about those boys."

"Thanks. I'm sure I could handle a few adolescent boys." His problem was one thirty-year-old man who was currently living way too close to the Last Chance for Regan's comfort. "I, uh, need to ask you about something."

"Sure."

"I hear there's a log-cabin rental just outside your fence line."

"Matter of fact, there is. We became better acquainted with that place a couple of winters ago when one of our hands chased a runaway horse over in that direction. He had to take refuge there. Do you want to rent it? I can put you in touch with the owner."

"No. I just need directions."

"Okay. Do you mind if I ask why?"

He hesitated. If he couldn't convince Drake to leave, word would get out sooner or later. The guy was bound to come into town. "Drake Brewster, my… former business partner, is staying there. He wants to see me."

Nick stroked his chin. "I see. I'm not sure it's safe to let you go over there by yourself, cowboy. I'd hate for you to get arrested for assault."

"Don't think it hasn't crossed my mind, but he's not worth it. He's here because he wants to salve his guilty conscience. If I can convince him he's wasting his time, I'm hoping he'll pack up and leave."

"And if he doesn't?"

Anger tightened Regan's gut. "I'll think of something else."

"Let me know what happens. Jack is friends with the owner of the cabin. If we put our heads together, we might come up with a way to get the guy evicted."

Regan smiled for the first time today. "Thanks. I always like a backup plan."

"Or, if the eviction idea isn't possible because of legal issues, Jack can send a work detail to that area with a few chain saws. They don't have to cut anything down, but they could make a hell of a noise. We could set up some battery-operated lights and start work around two in the morning."

"I like it." Regan chuckled. "Only thing is, if you drive a rat away from one hidey-hole, he's liable to take up residence somewhere else."

"Not in our town, he won't. Had I known about this cabin-rental deal, his sorry ass wouldn't be plunked down there, either. At the very least he'd be staying in Jackson, or even farther away in Cheyenne."

"I appreciate that sentiment more than I can say." Regan considered asking Nick to voice his sentiments to Lily, but then Nick would know things weren't great between them, and Regan wasn't ready to let that be public knowledge...yet.

"Want me to go with you?"

"No, but thanks for the offer. It means a lot."

"Just don't do anything stupid and slug him. Or if you do, make it look like an accident."

Regan was still laughing about that when the last

of the Chance vehicles left Peaceful Kingdom. He wouldn't mind telling Lily how Nick had responded to the news of Drake's sudden appearance. But that wouldn't be very mature of him, and besides, he didn't want to stir up trouble between those two friends over something that was his job to handle.

Lily had gone into the house to put away the bowls they'd used at the kids' craft table, and he considered whether it was time to lock the front gate. Then he noticed a truck and horse trailer coming down the road. All five horses had been picked up, but he hadn't kept track of everything going on. Maybe a sixth horse had been adopted and he hadn't heard about it. That would be great.

He headed over to find out, but the driver climbed out of the cab and made for the porch before he could get there. The guy knocked on the door and Lily let him in. Although Regan was curious, he knew that she didn't need him to come barging in as if he didn't think she could handle the situation.

Instead, he headed to the barn, where he knew there were chores waiting. Feeding time was coming up, and plenty of people had been in and out of the barn today. A few things would likely be out of place. Stall doors that should be open might be closed. Little stuff, but it could make feeding take longer.

Nick's support with the Drake issue had improved his mood considerably. He shouldn't be too hard on Lily for thinking the way she did. That was her nature, and her generosity of spirit was something he appreciated about her. He'd benefited from that every time they'd made love.

Sleeping down the hall the night before had been a

miserable experience he didn't want to repeat. So maybe they could agree to disagree about Drake and move on. Regan planned to pay Drake a visit tomorrow and talk him into leaving. The jerk had ruined one relationship for Regan, and damned if he was going to ruin another one by hanging around and providing a bone of contention between Regan and Lily.

Regan had just coiled a rope and hung it up when Lily came through the barn door leading a horse Regan had never seen before. He nudged back his hat in surprise. "Hello. Who's this?"

She stood holding the horse, which had a sorry-looking mane and tail and a dull, butterscotch-and-white coat. "His name is Taffy." She sounded defensive.

Regan had a sinking sensation that Lily had just accepted another horse mere hours after they'd cleared out five. They'd agreed that she wouldn't take in any more horses until she had an empty stall. "So what's Taffy doing here?"

She met his gaze, and defiance flashed in her blue eyes. "He has nowhere else to go."

He didn't doubt the guy who'd brought Taffy had said that. Whether it was true or not, Lily had clearly decided she was the only thing standing between Taffy and some horrible fate. He understood the impulse. But she had to get over it if she ever expected to make Peaceful Kingdom work the way it should.

Taking a deep breath, he chose his words carefully. "Is the owner still here?"

"No. And he lives in Montana, so if you're thinking he'll come back for Taffy, he won't."

"He brought this horse from *Montana*?"

"Yes."

Regan groaned. "Lily, your reputation for taking in horses is spreading fast. Out of the state, even. You can't keep doing this."

She swallowed. "I know. But I can't help it. So I have a big favor to ask of you. A huge favor. Would you live here until I can find a buyer to take over?"

"You mean live here with you? I'm already doing that."

She shook her head. "Not live here with me. I can't run this place. I might as well admit it and give up." Her voice trembled. "I realized when I was walking over here with Taffy that I've failed. I can't say no."

"You *can*. I know you can! Don't leave, Lily. These animals need you." *I need you.*

"And I'm going to let them down by taking in more! You can see that, right? This horse came all the way from Montana, and I took him."

"Because you weren't mentally prepared to say no. Think about all the other visualization techniques we've worked on together. You have to visualize the animals you have, and the space they need, and picture yourself saying no for the benefit of those already in your care."

She shook her head. "This isn't what I'm good at, Regan. I need to go back to Silicon Valley and design computer games."

"Don't say that." He felt sick to his stomach.

"I am saying it. Now if you'll excuse me, I'll take Taffy down to his stall. I'm putting him in with Sandy."

Stepping aside, he let her go by. He couldn't allow this terrible thing to happen, but he didn't know how to stop it. She didn't believe she could train herself to say no.

ONCE AGAIN, Lily spent the night alone in her bed. She and Regan had worked side by side handling the chores without talking. They both knew the routine and didn't need to talk, but the silence was nonetheless excruciating. Now they seemed to have nothing to say to each other.

How quickly everything had fallen apart. But the seeds of the destruction had been there all along. She couldn't be happy with a man who insisted on keeping his anger walled up inside and wouldn't take a golden opportunity to deal with the issue. His stubborn attitude regarding Drake could turn into a deal breaker for her.

Yet she'd been hopeful that he might change his mind and talk with his former friend. Maybe he just needed time to work up to it. But time had run out for her and Regan, because when faced with her first test of her new resolve to turn away a needy animal, she'd failed. She didn't belong here.

After tossing and turning all night, she managed to oversleep for the first time since she'd moved in. That just proved that she wasn't up to the job. Leaping out of bed, she threw on her clothes and barreled into the kitchen. The smell of coffee should have alerted her to the fact Regan was up, but she'd been too distracted to notice.

The coffeepot was turned off, but a thermos carafe that she kept handy for keeping her coffee warm was sitting on the counter next to a note.

Lily—
The critters are fed. I have an errand to run. See you in a few hours.
Regan

She tried to imagine what errand he'd have on a Sunday that would take a few hours, and then she remembered Drake. Regan had gone to see his former best friend to get him to leave Jackson Hole. Now that was depressing. She'd wanted them to talk, but not so they could widen the gulf between them.

Pouring herself a cup of coffee, she walked through the empty living room and down the hall past Regan's bedroom. She glanced in, and saw that he'd made his bed. It was a small thing, but it touched her that he was considerate enough to leave the room looking neat.

The third bedroom served as what she laughingly called an office. It contained her computer, a table and chair, and some cheap shelves for her books. When she moved out of this house, she'd be able to pack everything in half a day or less, which was typical for her.

While she waited for the computer to boot up, she thought about the email she was about to send expressing interest in the game-designing job. And she'd confirm that yes, she'd be willing to move back to Silicon Valley and work at the company's headquarters. She imagined the thrill of trading ideas with fellow gaming nerds. The game she'd written had been a solo effort with some consultation from Al, but it might be fun to brainstorm with others while she created more games.

It pretty much had to be fun because that was the option open to her. She sent the email and decided not to think about it any more today. Her next step involved contacting Morgan Chance, who was a real estate broker.

Yeah, well, she could do that later on. No rush. The process of selling this place would take a while. She was fairly sure Regan would agree to stay on until Morgan found a buyer. He'd handle Peaceful Kingdom so much better than she had. Maybe he'd consider buying it himself. That would be perfect.

Okay, maybe not perfect. Perfection was eluding her every time she reached for it. Fitting, then. It would be fitting if Regan bought this place. Whoever bought it would have to be tougher than she was. Maybe she should leave the person a list of other horse rescue organizations within driving distance.

An online search turned up a few, so she printed out a list. The new owner would have options to give anyone who came to the front gate. That would help ease the pain. She wasn't sure why she'd never thought of it. She'd been too busy getting ready for the adoption fair and making love to Regan, apparently.

Hunger finally drove her back to the kitchen. On her way through the living room, she looked out the front window and saw a truck pull up to the gate, which Regan would have locked behind him. Sure enough, the truck was hauling a horse trailer. She sincerely doubted the trailer was empty.

A stocky man got out of the driver's side and rattled the gate to see if it was locked. What if it hadn't been? Would he have driven in, unloaded his horse and left? Lily had experienced that once, and she'd felt sorry for a horse that had been unceremoniously dumped.

Something occurred to her that never had before. People were arriving without calling first. Her number was online, so they wouldn't have to go to a whole lot of trouble to get it. That would be the respectful way to handle the situation. So far, no one had done that. They'd simply shown up without checking to see if she had space.

As she thought about that, the Irish temper she'd inherited along with her red hair flared and began a slow burn. People had been taking advantage of her good nature. By allowing them to take advantage, she was imposing restrictions on the sweet animals she'd already accepted. She didn't have an animal problem. She had a people problem. She couldn't control how others behaved, but she could control her reaction to their behavior.

Returning to her office, she snatched up the list she'd printed and marched back through the living room and out the front door. The man was dressed like an average cowboy, but Lily had a high opinion of that label and she refused to assign it to this guy. He wanted to dump a horse without asking first. He was no cowboy.

She walked over to the gate. "Can I help you?"

"Yeah, I was told I could leave this horse with you. I wasn't sure how to get in. Good thing you came out."

"Who told you that you could leave a horse here?"

He waved a hand. "I dunno. Some guy I met in a coffee shop in Jackson. So, can you open the gate? I don't have a lot of time."

"Sorry, but I'm not opening the gate." She could hardly believe those words had come out of her mouth, but she was in a mood.

"How am I gonna get this horse inside?"

"You're not. I'm at capacity and can't accept any more horses."

"He's a good horse."

She steeled herself against thinking about the animal in the trailer. "I'm sure he is. But because I'm full, I can't take him." She rolled the list up and handed it over the gate. "You'll find several other options there."

He made an impatient noise low in his throat. "I don't want to go chasing all over the countryside."

She spared one moment of anguish for the horse stuck with such a subpar human being. But as Regan had suggested, she thought of the animals she already had in her care. They didn't deserve to be crowded because some idiot like this man showed up with another horse.

"So you really won't take him?" The guy seemed very disgusted.

"No." She stood there a moment and savored the sound of that word. "No, I won't." Then she turned and started back to the house.

But instead of going there, she found herself walking around the building and out to the new paddock. She counted, and all seventeen were there, including Taffy. Regan must have herded them in after he'd fed them breakfast.

She'd watched him do it several times before. Grabbing a fistful of mane, he'd vault onto whichever horse was handy. Then he'd ride bareback and use a coiled rope to direct the herd into the enclosure. He'd been poetry in motion. Suddenly she missed him with a deep, visceral ache. She wanted him to come home. She wanted to tell him that against all odds, she'd learned how to say no.

17

Regan parked in front of the little log cabin. He'd had to take a dirt road to get there, but the place sat all by itself in a clearing, so it had been simple to locate. Across the road ran a fence that marked the edge of Last Chance property. This rental was as close to the ranch as anyone could get without actually setting foot on it.

At least Drake had been smart enough to know he wouldn't be welcome at the Last Chance. Sarah welcomed nearly everyone who came to her door, but once Drake had introduced himself, he would have been sent on his way with a regal lift of Sarah's chin. Regan almost wished he had tried it, just so he could have experienced the Sarah Chance freeze-out.

Regan hadn't called ahead, either. Surprising Drake had a certain poetic justice to it after the way he'd startled the guy six months ago on Christmas Eve. Belatedly Regan wondered if Drake would have a woman with him. It was Sunday morning, and Drake could easily have gone into town last night in search of female companionship. What Drake sought, he usually found.

To hell with it. If he'd brought a woman home, so

what? She might want to know what kind of man she was dealing with, so Regan would be doing her a favor by barging in on their cozy setup. He banged on the front door.

A moment later it opened to reveal a man Regan barely recognized. Drake had always leaned toward the preppie look—clean-shaven, neat salon haircut, crisp white shirts and tailored slacks. This Drake had several days' growth of beard and was in desperate need of a good haircut. He wore a faded UV sweatshirt and jeans that had seen better days.

Drake blinked. Then his signature feature, green eyes that were once filled with mischief and laughter, widened. "You came." Gone was the cocky attitude. Well, mostly. He looked almost, but not quite, humble. "Thank you. Come in."

"Don't thank me yet, Brewster." Regan walked past him into the open floor plan that combined a kitchen with a living room. The kitchen looked relatively neat, but the living room was strewn with books and magazines. A half-full mug of coffee sat on an end table.

Checking over the reading material, Regan noticed quite a bit of motivational stuff, the kind of thing his parents loved. He even spotted *Happiness Is a Choice* by Bethany Grace. He'd met Bethany on several occasions. She and her husband, Nash Bledsoe, lived on a small ranch down the road from the Last Chance.

Regan would share none of that with Drake, however. Drake needed reasons to leave, not reasons to stick around and meet one of his favorite authors. Regan was prepared to give him those reasons to leave, preferably without bloodshed.

"I appreciate you coming so quickly." Drake moved some magazines off the couch. "Have a seat."

"I'll stand. The reason I came quickly is because I want you the hell out of my town."

"Sorry." Drake sank into an easy chair. "Not leaving. Not yet, anyway. It took me a week of hiking and hanging out in this cabin to work up the courage to call you. But I'm slowly figuring things out. I was right to come. Being here is exactly what I need."

"Yeah, well that's what it's always been about, isn't it? What *you* need. Let me tell you something, buddy." Regan pointed a finger at him. "Six months ago you broke up my engagement. Now, just by your presence, you're causing a problem with the new lady in my life. I'm not letting you screw with me twice in less than a year."

"Somebody new?" Drake's eyebrows rose. "That's terrific."

"It was, until you showed up. Now you've become an issue between us, and I won't have it." He hadn't thought he wanted to be here, but saying that to Drake's face felt damned good. Drake didn't have to know that Regan's relationship with Lily was shaky for any other reason but his presence.

"How can I be a problem? I don't even know her."

"And you won't, if I have anything to say about it. I can't trust you around my girlfriends, remember?"

Drake's expression grew bleak. "Oh, I remember, all right. It was the low point of my life."

"It was no walk in the park for me, either, asshole."

"I'm sure it wasn't." Drake gazed at him. "I'll never be able to make it up to you, either."

"You've got that right."

Drake swept an arm around the room. "As you can see, I've done some reading in the past week."

"Yeah. So what?"

"I'm serving as my own therapist, which is always dicey, but near as I can tell, I was jealous and couldn't admit it to myself. So I acted like an idiot."

"Jealous? You wanted Jeannette?" He remembered what Lily had asked. Maybe he had missed the obvious, after all.

"No, I didn't want Jeannette. I wanted something you had. I wanted your…your self-confidence."

"My *what?*"

"Don't pretend you don't know what I'm talking about. You've always had that basic knowledge of who you are and what you want. You went to that Buck Brannaman clinic and you got it instantly, whereas I just faked it. You're ten times the vet I am." He held Regan's gaze. "I've been pea-green with envy since day one, O'Connelli."

Regan stared at him in stunned silence. If he'd had a million years to analyze the situation, he never would have come up with that.

"You want some coffee?"

"Yeah. Guess so." He walked over to the couch and sat down. Moments later, Drake handed him a mug of hot coffee, and he took it with a nod of thanks.

He used the familiarity of sipping coffee to buy himself some time and gather his thoughts. At last he had something of a handle on what Drake had confessed, but he was confused. "What you're saying makes no sense. You were the one with all the important connections. I was the poor kid on a scholarship. You belonged in that world. Your parents guaranteed our clinic would be a huge success. You had everything. I was riding on your coattails the whole time."

"Nope. Not true. I had the connections, but you had the grades. I had the trust-fund money, but you had the difficult-to-define qualities of a great vet. I needed you. If I'd tried to go it alone, I would have failed. I don't have the genius for the profession that you do. For your information, I got somebody else to fill your spot, but they don't have your skill. The clinic's about to go under."

Regan frowned. "I'm sorry." Surprisingly, he was. He'd put a lot of himself into building that practice, and he hated to think of it dying.

"It shouldn't survive. I'm not cut out for the profession. I'm a huge disappointment to my parents, but they've always suspected you were propping me up. Two weeks ago I told them why you left. I'll be surprised if they don't disinherit me." He shrugged. "And amazingly, I don't give a shit."

"What are you going to do?"

"That's what I'm here to find out. Until now, other people have told me what I'm supposed to want. I need to figure out what I actually want." He glanced at Regan. "But that's not why I asked you to come and see me. I crapped all over your relationship with Jeannette. I know sorry doesn't cut it, but short of giving you a kidney, I don't know what else I can do but say that I'm deeply sorry. That's not how you treat a friend."

Regan grinned, which shocked the hell out of both of them, judging from Drake's expression. "A kidney? You'd give me a kidney?"

And just like that, the tension eased. The old familiar spark was back in Drake's eyes. "You might not want it, dude. I boozed it up pretty good in college. But if you need one, I'm there for you."

"I'll keep that in mind. You never know."

"So what about this new lady? What's she like?"

"Terrific, but there are problems." Regan thought one might be solved, but she might require evidence. Maybe if she was blown away by his renewed friendship with Drake, she'd listen to his ideas about learning to say no. "Would you like to meet her?"

Drake froze. "That would be okay with you?"

"Sure." Regan gave him the evil eye. "But if I ever think, for one second, that you would—"

"God, no. I've worked too hard to fix this mess." He rubbed his chin. "Guess I should shave first, huh?"

"I should probably present you like this, just to guarantee she won't take a shine to you, but as a measure of my faith in your trustworthiness, yeah, why don't you shave?"

By LATE MORNING, Lily still hadn't contacted Morgan about listing the property. She kept finding other things to do. She made a sign, which she'd have laminated before she left, but she hung it on the front gate for now because a sign was definitely called for. If it looked like rain, she'd bring it in. It read: "Sorry, but our barn is at capacity. Please take a flier for other options."

To go along with the sign, she planned to install an information tube at the gate and keep it stocked with copies of the list she'd made up earlier this morning. She'd posted a prominent notice on the website requiring a phone call in advance of bringing a horse to Peaceful Kingdom. But because of her previous lax policy, people still might drive up to the gate unannounced and expect to drop off a horse. She didn't want a future owner to have to deal with that.

On impulse, she spent some time out in the paddock, loving on the horses, and some more time with Wilbur and Harley, and even a few minutes talking to the chickens. She'd miss all those critters. And not just a little bit, either. She'd miss them as if she'd suddenly developed a hole in her heart. Somewhere during her tour of the place, she began to reconsider her decision to leave.

After all, she'd turned away a horse. She'd come up with a list of alternative rescue operations, she'd posted a notice on the website and she'd made a sign to hang on the gate. The fence company had set up physical boundaries that made her life easier. But she'd needed some mental boundaries, and now she had them.

At last she stood in front of her green-and-orange house and admired the flowers blooming their little hearts out. Someone new might repaint, and that didn't sit well with her. They might forget to water the flowers. They might not love potbellied pigs.

Spreading her arms wide, she twirled around. "I'm staying!" she shouted at the top of her lungs. "You hear me, horses, pigs and chickens? I'm staying!"

About that time Regan's truck pulled up to the gate, and her bubble of happy optimism burst. She didn't want to hear how he'd chewed out his best friend and ordered him to leave Jackson Hole. She loved Regan, but if he insisted on clutching that anger to his heart, then… Her breath caught. She *loved* him? Well, of course she did. That's why she was so upset with him for the way he was handling his problem with Drake.

She waited as he unlocked the gate, got back in his truck and drove into the yard. Wait a minute. Someone was in the passenger seat. Her heart began pounding. If that man was who she thought he was, then maybe all was not lost.

The guy got out. His coffee-colored hair was on the longish side, but after years at Berkeley, she was used to that look. He was wearing a ratty old college sweatshirt and scruffy jeans with sneakers. That also reminded her of Berkeley. He had on shades that looked remarkably like the ones Regan used to wear. Maybe he needed protection, too.

Regan walked toward her, his smile hopeful. "Lily, I'd like you to meet Drake Brewster."

Her chest tightened. Regan had done it. He'd accepted his best friend's apology, and then he'd brought him home to her as a peace offering.

Turning to the man who had betrayed Regan, she wondered how much courage he'd required to come here and ask for forgiveness. Quite a bit, probably. She held out her hand. "I'm happy to meet you, Drake Brewster."

"Same here, ma'am." He took off his shades to reveal startling green eyes. "Regan's told me a lot about you." His accent made him sound like a plantation owner from *Gone with the Wind*.

"Oh? Like what?"

"That you're brilliant, and generous, and beautiful. Just between you and me, I think the guy's in love with you."

"Hey!" Regan frowned at Drake, but his mouth twitched at the corners, as if he might be holding back laughter. "Don't go poking your nose in my business."

Drake shrugged. "Just makin' an observation."

"Well, go observe somewhere else, okay? Take a

stroll around the property or something. I need to talk to Lily privately."

Drake placed a hand on his chest in exaggerated shock. "Lord, boy! Are you telling me to get lost when I just got here? Where I come from, that's not how we treat our guests. No, sir."

"Okay, then go in the house and make yourself some coffee. Have a beer. Have a mint julep. Sheesh. I'd forgotten you were such a pain in the ass."

"Okay. I'll leave. But don't louse this up. She's obviously a find. Close the deal, boy, or mark my words, you'll regret it for the rest of your life."

Lily watched them with wonder and a bubbling kind of joy. Men didn't joke around like that unless they were close. As for the topic of conversation, that sent excitement skittering through her.

"Advice appreciated. Now git."

With a martyred sigh, Drake trudged off toward the house.

Regan turned back to Lily, his expression tender. Nudging back his hat, he closed the distance between them. "I saw the sign on the gate."

"I put that up after I turned away a horse."

His eyebrows lifted. "You did what?"

"I figured that whoever took over didn't need yet another horse to deal with. Besides, the guy had some nerve, just driving up to my gate without calling ahead. But FYI, you can't take over, because I'm staying."

"Is that so?" His mouth twitched again, as if he was having trouble holding back a grin. "Does that mean you don't need me anymore?"

"Oh, I need you." That came across with a little more

emotion than she'd intended, but her feelings were running high at the moment.

He drew her into his arms. "Good, because I need you. And an FYI for you, Brewster totally jumped the gun, but he was right. I'm madly in love with you."

Joy thrummed through her as she looped her arms around his neck. "How convenient. I just discovered that I'm madly in love with you, too."

He pulled her in tight. "So what are we going to do about that?"

"Nothing right now. We have a guest."

"So we do. Damn. I brought him as Exhibit A, but I forgot about the fact that he'd stick around."

The screen door opened. "Have you proposed yet, genius?"

"Go back in the house, Brewster!"

"Better get on with it." The door banged shut.

Regan looked into her eyes. "He ruined the suspense."

"I don't care." If he weren't holding on to her, she might lift up into the sky like a helium balloon. She was just that happy.

"Will you marry me, Lily King?"

"Yes. Yes, I will."

The screen door creaked open again. "How about now? Have you accomplished what you came to do?"

Regan sighed. "I have one more important thing to take care of. I'm going to kiss this woman until her eyes roll back in her head. You might want to give us some privacy for that."

"Nothing doing. I'm going to watch."

"Suit yourself." Regan lowered his mouth to hers.

At first she felt a little embarrassed that Drake was

standing on the porch taking it all in, but then she forgot about him. She forgot about everything but the explosive pleasure of kissing Regan O'Connelli. And if anyone were to ask, she'd happily confirm that her eyes really did roll back in her head.

* * * * *

Think Drake deserves another chance?
Read on for a sneak peek of
RIDING HARD,
the next SONS OF CHANCE
book by Vicki Lewis Thompson
coming July 2014
from Harlequin Blaze!

Tracy wondered if the mare was still hungry. After all, she was eating for two. What Tracy knew about such things would fit inside a bottle cap. She really did need Drake's advice.

As if her thoughts had conjured him up, she heard him enter the barn, his boot heels clicking on the wooden floor. She hurried over to the stall door and glanced quickly down the aisle. Sunlight streamed into the barn, outlining his manly physique in gold. He'd taken to wearing Western clothes recently, and they suited him. Boy, did they ever suit him.

She needed to gather her wits, so she didn't call out to him. Hoping he hadn't noticed her, she went back to brushing Dottie. For someone who had vowed to remain cool and distant, she sure had a lot of heat pouring through her veins. She drew in a deep breath and let it out slowly.

"Tracy? Are you in here?" His rich voice echoed in the rafters. "Down here, last stall on the left." Damn, but her hands were shaking. This was not good.

"Thanks. I tried the house, but you didn't answer the

door." His footsteps came closer. "My eyes aren't quite adjusted to the light."

She glanced up, and there he was, six-foot-something of testosterone-fueled male. His Western shirt emphasized the breadth of his shoulders. He wasn't wearing a cowboy hat, and she didn't think she'd ever seen him wearing one. She wondered about that. Most cowboy wannabes couldn't wait to show up in a hat.

When he opened the stall door, she realized her mistake. Jumpiness aside, she should have walked out to meet him. Then she could have let him go in the stall alone. Instead he was about to come in with her.

Unless she engineered a little do-si-do with him and then made her escape looking like a frightened rabbit, she was stuck here. Her three-foot limit was about to be violated, and she didn't know what to do about it.

REQUEST YOUR FREE BOOKS!
2 FREE NOVELS PLUS 2 FREE GIFTS!

♦ HARLEQUIN®
Blaze®
red-hot reads!

HB13R2

Double Exposure

by Erin McCarthy...

Emma shifted on the seat of Kyle's car, hoping she wasn't smearing paint onto the upholstery. Why on earth had she volunteered to do this stupid group photo shoot? With the coworker she secretly craved, no less? The sooner she got this paint off and some clothes on, the sooner sanity would reappear.

"Can I take a shower at your place?" Maybe properly clothed she would be less aware of Kyle and her reaction to him. Because she could not, would not—ever—indulge herself with Kyle. Dating and sex made people emotional and irrational. It didn't mix with work.

"Of course you can." Kyle pulled out of the parking lot for the short trip to his place.

She caught sight of herself in the visor mirror. She looked worse than she'd thought. There was no way Kyle would ever come near her like this. Her hair was shot out in all directions, and her skin was emerald-green, with the whites of her eyes and her teeth gleaming in contrast. The napkins she'd used to cover herself tufted up from her chest. "I look like a frog eating barbecue!"

Kyle started laughing so hard he ended up coughing.

"It's not funny!" she protested.

Before they could debate that, he turned in to his building. Still chuckling, he ushered her toward the stairs. "What a day." He tossed his keys onto the table inside the entry of his apartment. "Bathroom's this way. Come on."

Emma followed, her eyes inevitably drawn to his tight butt. He was muscular in an athletic, natural way. Her fingers itched to squeeze all that muscle.

"I'm really good at keeping secrets, you know." Kyle turned, his eyes dark and unreadable.

She was suddenly aware of the sexual tension between them. They were mostly naked, standing inches apart. His mouth was so close....

"If anything happens here today, you can be sure it will never be mentioned at the office."

"What could happen?" She knew what he meant, but she needed to hear confirmation that he was equally attracted to her.

"This." Kyle closed the gap between them.

Emma didn't hesitate, but let her eyes shut as his mouth covered hers in a deep, tantalizing kiss.

Pick up DOUBLE EXPOSURE by Erin McCarthy, available wherever you buy Harlequin® Blaze® books.